The
Autum
VOLUME
TWO
Woo

By

KURT BUSIEK
WRITER

and

BENJAMIN DEWEY
ARTIST

JORDIE BELLAIRE
COLORS

JOHN ROSHELL *of* COMICRAFT
DESIGN & LETTERING

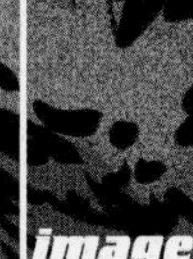

FOR BENJAMIN DEWEY:
LINDSAY ELLIS
Production Assistant

FOR JORDIE BELLAIRE:
JEONG JOO PARK &
CHAN SOO *of* YESFLAT
Flatters

FOR COMICRAFT:
JIMMY BETANCOURT
Lettering

RICHARD STARKINGS
President & First Tiger

REPRESENTATION:
LAW OFFICES OF HARRIS M. MILLER II, P.C.
rights.inquiries@gmail.com

THE AUTUMNLANDS Volume Two: WOODLAND CREATURES. First printing. February 2017. Published by Image Comics, Inc. Office of publication: 2701 NW Vaughn St., Suite 780, Portland, OR 97210. Printed in the USA. For information regarding the CPSIA on this printed material call: 203-595-3636 and provide reference #RICH–724112. For international rights, contact: foreignlicensing@imagecomics.com. ISBN: 978-1-63215-713-3.

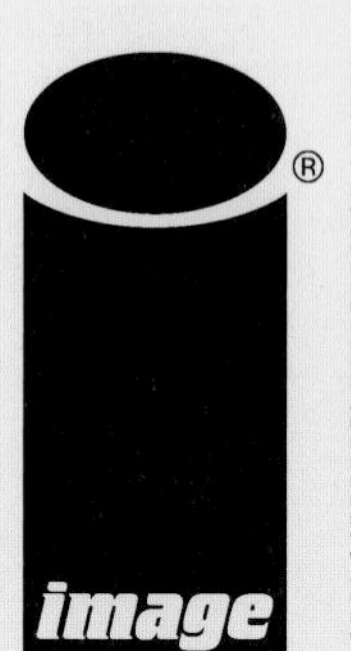

One

I DID NOT KNOW WHAT HAD HAPPENED –
– TO ENNA, REG, KEV, LADY GHARTA, THE SURVIVING FOLK OF KENEIL.
I JUST KNEW THEY'D BEEN RESCUED. AND THAT WAS ALL THAT MATTERED –
Anyone wounded or ill, bring them to the medical plaza!
We'll bring around hot soup and watered wine in short order!
...and punitive measures against all the bison tribes will be brought up in the Great Council soon...
Why didn't you come sooner?
What, you hadn't heard? No, of course you wouldn't have...
You! HAH! You belong in jail – and I'll see you sentenced!
Sandorst is the hero here! Sandorst, Third Councillor of –
Sandorst, lack-witted, spell-mangling fool!
You dare?
Dare? I haven't even begun to –

The Time Betw

by Ergeret Obria

Peace reigned on the broad decks of the rescue hall Sarabarr the Merciful.

The long ordeal was over. The Great Champion and the wizards of Keneil had staved off the ravening bison hordes, holding them at bay until deliverance could arrive.

Now they could finally rest, wizards and commoners alike. Could tend their wounds and discomforts and think back on all they had lost. Friends. Family. Treasures and possessions that had taken lifetimes to amass. And for too many, all sense of safety.

A city had fallen. The smallest and most rustic of the Seventeen Cities Above the Plain, but a city nonetheless. Thousands had died, in

the crash or in the siege that followed.

They'd sought to work a miracle, these wizards, when they cast a spell so intricate, vast and all-consuming that it drained Keneil's levitation spells, sent it plummeting to Earth. They'd sought to reach through time itself, to bring back the Great Champion, with hopes of reversing the long decline of magic throughout the Autumnlands.

And they'd succeeded. They'd retrieved the Champion, though if he could restore magic, none could say.

But he'd saved them, at least. And at long last, they knew, their world would be calm and uneventful once more.

Or so they believed...

...ridiculous! The bison would have fled the moment they saw the rescue hall arriving! They were no match for the mages aboard!
Gharta. Gharta, your heart...
You did nothing! Nothing but risk our security at every turn — and endanger everyone!

Pff. I'd always heard warthogs were a foolish and unintelligent race, but I didn't know it was this glaring.
Endanger? If not for my heroic actions — in the face of great peril and the barest trickles of magic, I might add —

I warn you, "barn owl," there is no lack of magic here.
If you want to test your soft city skills against mine...
Guards! Guards!
Mad-creature!

Father, Lady Gharta! Don't — please don't fight!
Dusty's still down below! We have to turn back! There's still a chance to —

SILENCE, all of you!
...s-save...?

L-l-lord *Tallon!*

You will give me your full accounts of all that transpired on the ground — and *prior* to the fall. We will discuss it —

— *including* the disobedience of all the involved wizards. But that will be later.

For now, we have other concerns. You will come with me, Lady Gharta. There are urgent matters before us.

Her?! B-but she — she's the ringleader! Along with the coyote! They should both be —

You may come too, Councillor Sandorst. This concerns Telm as well.

Wh-what —

I am told you may have actually conjured the Great Champion, Seeker. If so, we require his aid as well.
Where is he?
Pfah! There's no way he's the real —

The Champion is... no longer among us, Lord Tallon.
And I fear...

"...HE MAY NO LONGER BE AMONG THE *LIVING,* EITHER."

huh
huhh

nnnhh

THROUGH IT ALL, THE *BRIDGE COLLAPSE,* THE RAPIDS, THE ROCKS – HE'D HELD ONTO HIS *SWORD.* BUT HE WASN'T *BREATHING.*
WAS HE DEAD? I DIDN'T *KNOW.* NOR WHAT TO DO IF HE WASN'T.

I HADN'T BEEN *TRAINED* FOR –
koff
k-koff

Oh, thank the gods! Thank you, each and every one!
The bridge, sir. I couldn't — but Sandorst *blew up* the bridge, and you and Seven-Scars fell —
— and I went after you but —

Quiet, kid.

There.

Gone. But where?
Will he — is he coming after us?
Maybe. Not tonight, though, I bet.

He'd need to ford the river, and we're miles away from anywhere safe.
And he'd have to get reinforcements, too.
We'll be good for tonight.

WE TREATED HIS *SHOULDER* WITH MOSS HE FOUND AND SOME HERBS. WASHED A LOINCLOTH AS WELL AS WE COULD.
THEN WE GATHERED WOOD AND I LIT A *FIRE* –
So what do we do? I can't send a beacon to the cities – I only know a few spells, even if we had the magic to draw on.
Do we stay by the river, wait for a search party?
No.

We get outta here at first light. I don't know if they're sendin' any search parties...
...but Seven-Scars knows where we are. So I'm leavin'.

But –
Look, kid, you don't want to come along, you don't fuckin' *have* to. I appreciate you pullin' me out of the drink...
...but I didn't *ask*, did I?

You – you'd –

Oh, don't make that face at me, kid. I'm immune.
You make your own choices, that's all I'm saying.

I can't tell you what to do. Come with me, go your own way, up to you. You been growin' up fast.
So think like a grown-up.

O-okay.
Then tell me something.

You're the *Great Champion.* You're the hero who unleashed magic into the world, millennia ago.
All those spells they cast when they brought you here say you're him, that they got the right one.
So what did you *do?*

I got no fuckin' clue, kid.

I was a soldier. The world was at war. We had a mission.
I remember waking up in my rack that morning, freezing.
I remember joining up with my team...
I don't remember anything else. I wish I did. I've been wrackin' my brains, but...
Nothing? Nothing at all?
Could it have been the spell?
Shit, I still don't know this isn't all some painkiller-induced hallucination, kid.
Let's catch some shut-eye while we can.
SO WE SLEPT.
OR *HE* SLEPT.
I TRIED TO GET COMFORTABLE, HALF-COLD, HALF-WARM, ON *DIRT* AND *ROCK.* AND TRIED TO MAKE SENSE OF ALL THAT HAD BEEN HAPPENING.

AND EVENTUALLY, I SLEPT AS WELL, WITH NO NEW WISDOM.
AT DAYBREAK, HE CHOSE US A PATH *WESTWARD.* I ASKED WHY THAT ONE.
HE DIDN'T ANSWER.

Okay. Can I ask another question?
Hnh.

You, um, killed those bison soldiers. The ones waiting in ambush.
Sure. They would have killed everyone there.

It's just — in the Cities — well, they'd call that brutal. Uncivilized.
If anything like that were to happen, first it would be debated, brought before the city leaders.
And if it *had* to happen...

...it'd be done with as much kindness as possible...
Debate? Kindness? You don't get it, kid. There wasn't time for any of that. They'd attacked once, they were gonna do it again.
Fuck, kid, don't you have *wars* around here?

Um...we've had wars. But those are like, in the stories. In olden times.
Not anymore.

You're shittin' me.
What, not *anywhere?*

I don't...think so. Not in the Cities, at least.
Or anywhere below them...

Huh.
Crazy fuckin' world.
HE SOUNDED...*WISTFUL.* I DIDN'T UNDERSTAND.

WHY WOULD THE *GREAT CHAMPION,* THE HERO OF ALL THE BEST LEGENDS, THE MOST *GLORIOUS* WARRIOR IN ALL HISTORY...
...WHY WOULD HE FEEL THAT WAY ABOUT *OUR* TIMES?
I WOULD HAVE *ASKED,* BUT I DID NOT THINK HE'D RESPOND.

WE HADN'T EATEN SINCE THE MORNING BEFORE, SO WE GATHERED *FOOD.* THE LOCAL FAUNA WAS SCARCE –

– AND HE DIDN'T TRUST THEM NOT TO UP AND START *TALKING* TO HIM, HE SAID.

AS FOR FRUITS AND OTHER PLANTS, I KNEW NEXT TO NOTHING, BUT –

Yeah, *this'll* be okay.

That... is that magic?

Hand me that leafy shit, will you?

AND SO –
Tell me about magic.
Huh?
You've been asking questions. Now it's my turn. If I'm supposed to reload all this shit, what is it? How does it work?

Um...the way my father explained it...
There's power – *hatsas* – in everything. Wind, flesh, stone, everything. All the world is suffused with it.

What magic does – it's a way to tap into it. To concentrate it, control it –
What, mentally?

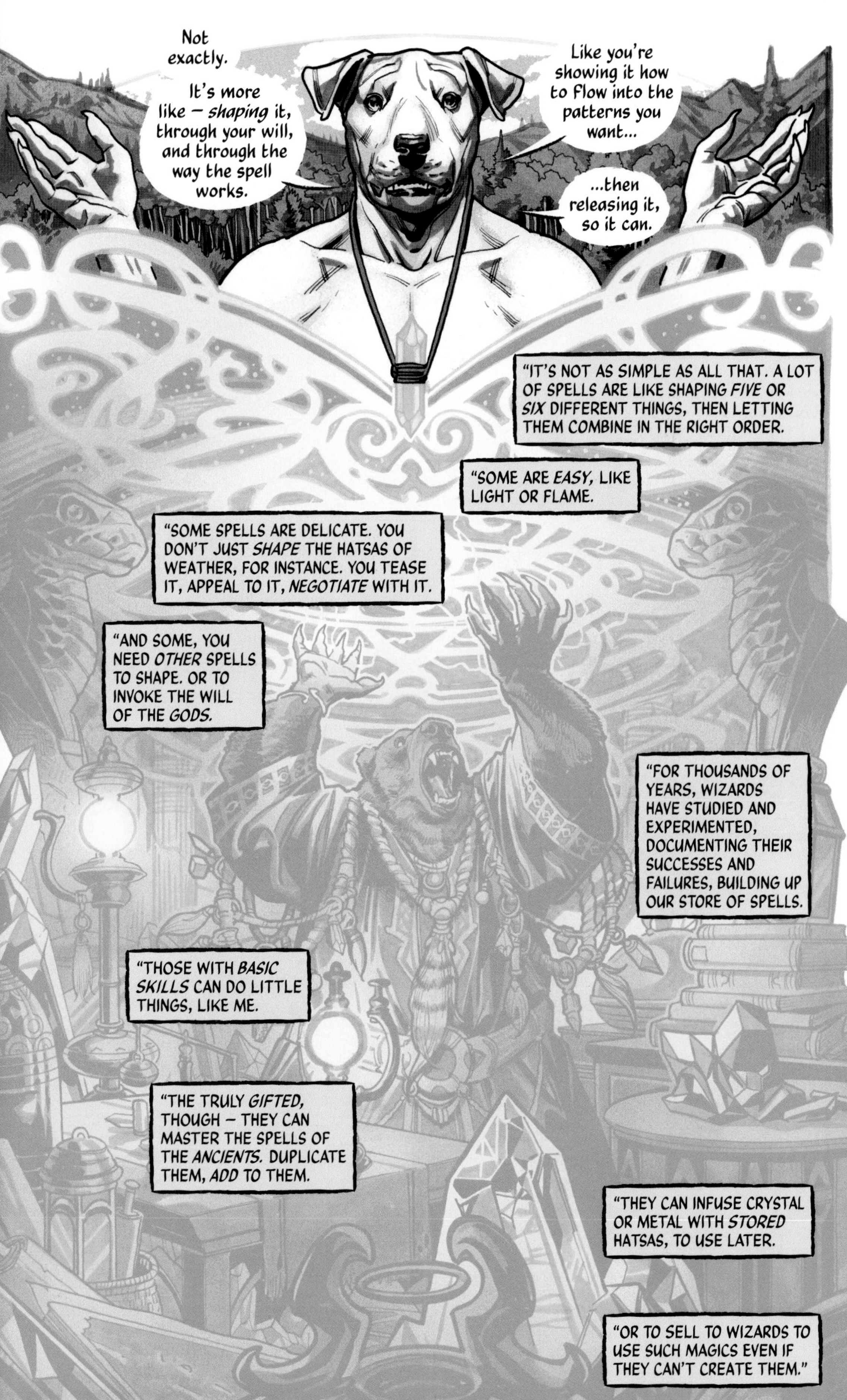

Not exactly.
It's more like — *shaping* it, through your will, and through the way the spell works.
Like you're showing it how to flow into the patterns you want...
...then releasing it, so it can.
"IT'S NOT AS SIMPLE AS ALL THAT. A LOT OF SPELLS ARE LIKE SHAPING *FIVE* OR *SIX* DIFFERENT THINGS, THEN LETTING THEM COMBINE IN THE RIGHT ORDER.
"SOME ARE *EASY,* LIKE LIGHT OR FLAME.
"SOME SPELLS ARE DELICATE. YOU DON'T JUST *SHAPE* THE HATSAS OF WEATHER, FOR INSTANCE. YOU TEASE IT, APPEAL TO IT, *NEGOTIATE* WITH IT.
"AND SOME, YOU NEED *OTHER* SPELLS TO SHAPE. OR TO INVOKE THE WILL OF THE *GODS.*
"FOR THOUSANDS OF YEARS, WIZARDS HAVE STUDIED AND EXPERIMENTED, DOCUMENTING THEIR SUCCESSES AND FAILURES, BUILDING UP OUR STORE OF SPELLS.
"THOSE WITH *BASIC SKILLS* CAN DO LITTLE THINGS, LIKE ME.
"THE TRULY *GIFTED,* THOUGH — THEY CAN MASTER THE SPELLS OF THE *ANCIENTS.* DUPLICATE THEM, *ADD* TO THEM.
"THEY CAN INFUSE CRYSTAL OR METAL WITH *STORED* HATSAS, TO USE LATER.
"OR TO SELL TO WIZARDS TO USE SUCH MAGICS EVEN IF THEY CAN'T CREATE THEM."

Uh-huh. And now this stuff, this hot sauce – it's fading away?
Hatsas. And yes. There is less of it every year.
It's still in everything, and suffuses everything, but thinly. It takes more work every season to gather what we need for our spells.

Our world...it was once known as the Summerlands, long before my time. Before the Cities, even.
Magic was plentiful, and miracles abounded.
But now we're in the Autumnlands. And winter is around the corner.

Huh.
And I =krnch= did this.

And you don't remember.
I don't remember.

KAARK

What the – ?

Kaark.
God-killer.
Kaark.

The fuck was *that* thing?
I...I don't know. I've never seen anything like it. Never *heard* of anything like it.

HRRMBBL
W-wh...?
Huh? Learoyd, why –

What? What? Learoyd, what's going on?
It – it's right –

Come on, Dusty. Don't fuckin' play games with me. You didn't...didn't see that? Didn't hear that?
Hear...?

I didn't see anything. There was that weird bird, and then you just staggered, and –
What? What did you see?

Huh.
Okay. Let's go.

AND WE WENT ON.
AND I TRIED TO HAVE FAITH.
HE WAS THE GREAT CHAMPION, AND I TRIED TO HAVE FAITH –

Two

What Walks These Hills

by Targeenan Tem

It was the hum he'd been listening for. A hum made by no earthly being, one that filled the soul with thoughts of peace and soft rain and far-off, flickering lightning.

He listened until he felt it. And then followed.

And there, in the clearing below, he found it.

It was no sky-yacht, no rich wizard's toy, nor even the great luxury-craft of the indolent lords to the south. None could afford it, and if they could, of what would they have built it?

The wood was finer-grained and more lustrous than any found in forests known to the civilized tribes. The gleaming brasswork—if brass it was at all—iridescent and hypnotic, like the gleaming shell of some beautiful, exotic insect, dappled in undersea light. The delicate inlays, the silks, the smell of it, like coriander and the memory of woodfire.

And the machineries. As large and powerful as anything in an ocean-spanning freighter that creaked and groaned with the force of the upper winds, yet these meshed so smoothly their movements felt like liquid, like poetry. It walked, rather than sailed—he had seen it walk, with his own eyes—with that hum of forgotten storms and evening solace.

Now it lay below, couched like some slumbering predator, waiting, wary, one eye half-lidded for danger.

And the woman...

ILLUSTRATED BY INTUS PARRA

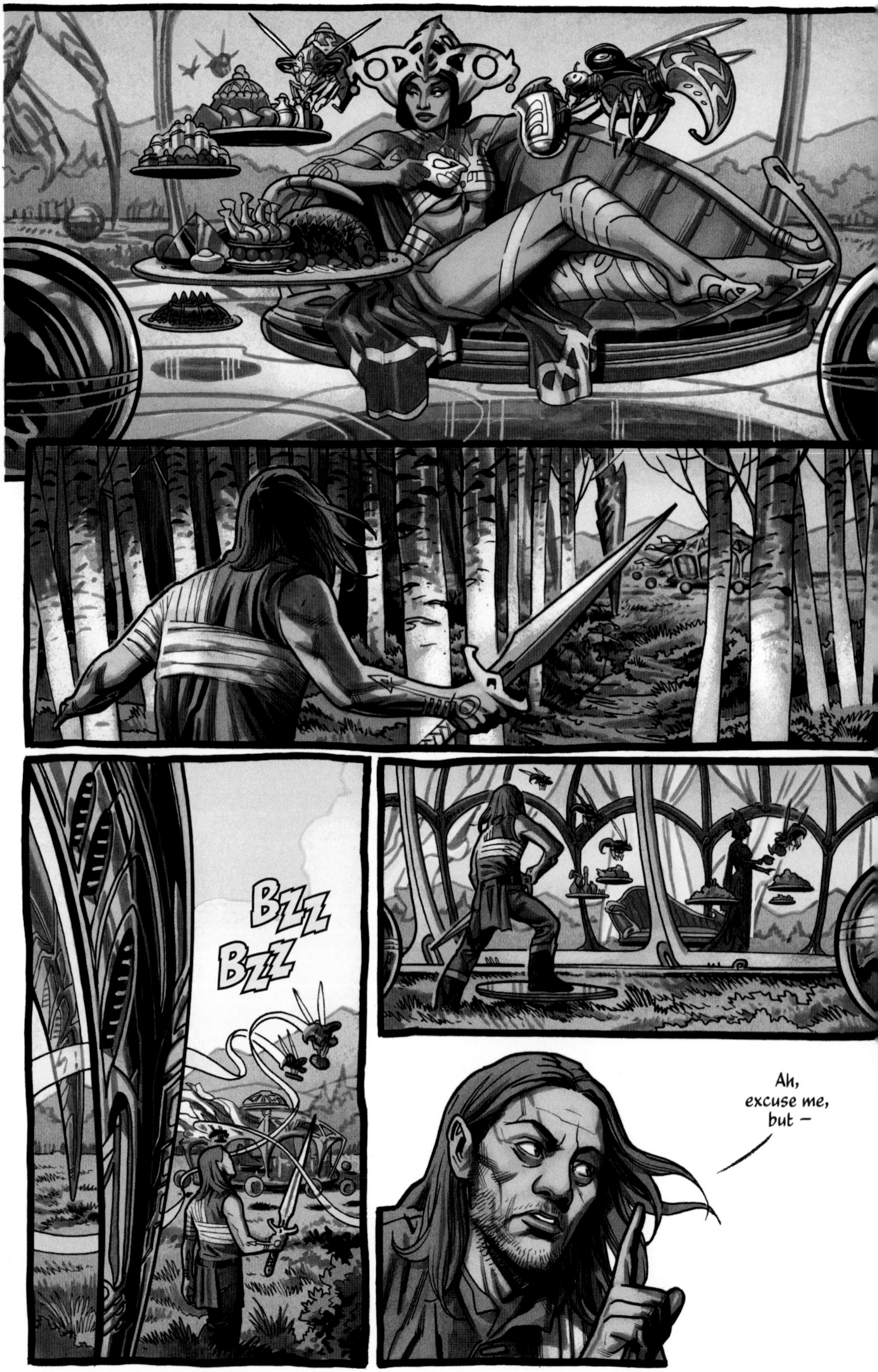

BZZ
BZZ

Ah, excuse me, but –

OHHHHHH!!
You — you —

Hooph. You startled the life out of me, I swear. Don't *do* that!
I didn't mean to. I just —
Goodness, but you're a fit fellow, aren't you? One of McCready's field boys? Newly promoted, maybe?
Not that I'd know if you'd been active for years, of course —

— I haven't been back to Central in a good century, I think. Maybe more.
Look, sorry if I —
I've been so *utterly* out of touch.

You've been interacting with the tribes, haven't you? Not supposed to do any of that these days, I hear.
I'm —
And *wounded,* too!

Careless, I suppose — you new actives always are, at first. Beta-beta! *Attend* him!
Wait — what —
Oh, don't be a baby.

Can I ask what –
BZZZZZ
Oh, McCready would *like* that, wouldn't he? Always with his nose in.
No, no, no. Do I ask why I didn't sense your approach? Why my sectroids didn't alert to you?

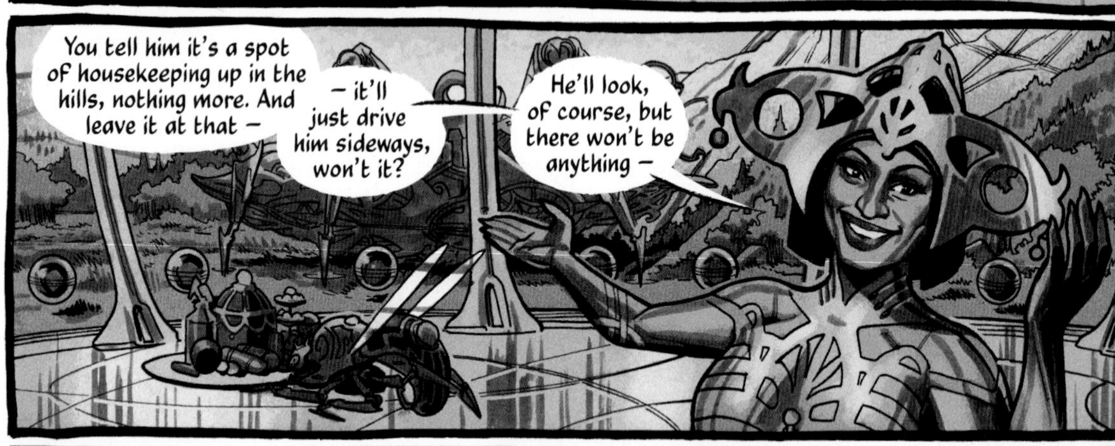
You tell him it's a spot of housekeeping up in the hills, nothing more. And leave it at that –
– it'll just drive him sideways, won't it?
He'll look, of course, but there won't be anything –

That's odd. It can't seem to lock on and re-knit your tissues. Even shielded, you're close enough so that shouldn't matter.
BZB ZB ZUBB
Have to have him checked out by Belcastro one of these decades.

Still, at least I can do something about those rags you're wearing, hm?
Epsie!
If my eye is still at all good at judging a man's sizes – and I think it is –
– well, here, try these on. You'll be warmer, I dare say.
But –
No buts. And don't mind me, I've seen it all. Hop, *hop!*

Fit *well*, do they?
Y...yes, but –
No buts, no buts. Happy to help.

Got to go. *So* much to do. Finish the breakfast, why don't you? Hate to see it go to waste.
But –
Oh, stop. You sound like a pulp-sorter.

Busy busy *busy!* Things here may hold a few days, and it's isolated anyway, isn't it? Got greater crises in the Ramblelands.
Won't wait.
Hey! What the –
See you at a Gather-In, perhaps, if I ever make it to another!

My best to McCready!
And you clean up quite nicely, by the way!
The fuck is going –

McCready?
Belcastro?
Hnh!
Heavy –

...
Huh.

Learoyd! Hey, *Learoyd!*

So here's where you got to. When I woke up, I figured you were out rounding up something to eat.
But where'd you get the clothes? And where'd you find...

...is that *jewelfruit?*
I...don't know. Probably. If that's what it looks like.

Learoyd, what's going on? Your clothes, this food...
Dusty...

I wish to hell you knew. Then you could explain it to *me.*
HE WAS *DISTRACTED.* NOT FULLY THERE, WITH ME. HIS MIND WAS...
...IT WAS WHEREVER IT HAD BEEN THE DAY *BEFORE,* WHEN HE HAD SEEN AND HEARD SOMETHING *UTTERLY INVISIBLE* TO ME.

WE SAT, AND ATE. IT WAS *DELICIOUS.*
THERE WERE FOODS THERE I'D ONLY *HEARD* ABOUT. FOODS I HAD NO IDEA WHAT THEY *WERE.*
AND ALL OF IT FRESH AND WARM – OR COLD – AS WOULD BE BEST. BUT WHERE IT *CAME* FROM –

Dusty, you say you've never seen anyone who looked like me before. No humans? None at all?
None. Why?

None at all... Huh.
HE DIDN'T *EXPLAIN.* HE RARELY *DID,* NOT BACK THEN.

AND WE KEPT GOING. HIGHER AND *HIGHER* –
SNOW!

Yeah, and not the last we'll see, I bet. Look, you need the cloak? You don't even have a shirt...
No, no –

– it'd have to get a lot worse for a terrier to feel it.
My father always says dogs are the best suited of the tribes to travel the world.
He says it's because we're so –

– um – I mean – he said –

S-sorry. I just –

Sounds like your father was a smart m – terrier. I'm sure you miss him.

Th-thanks...

Sometimes I f-forget. And then when I remember again, it's...

...hm?

What?

There's something...that way. Like a great source of *hatsas* – magic – but not quite.
Up the mountains.
Does it feel anything like that clearing? This morning?
Is it moving?

No. No, there was nothing there this morning. Just you and the food.
Why –

Hnh.

Hnnn...

Dammit.

What? *What?*
Nothing. Let's just keep moving.

NO.
Are we headed somewhere, Learoyd? Are we *looking* for something? *Tell* me.
Hm?
You know what we're doin', kid.

We're gettin' away from that goddamn river, is what we're doin'. It's bison territory.
See? All the valleys leading east, they all lead back to the river. We have to find a pass west, through the mountains...
...find valleys leading somewhere else, streams that flow to *other* goddamn rivers. That's all.

But...if you sense anything else, magic or not-magic, let me know. We don't want any surprises.
HE WASN'T TELLING ME THE TRUTH, AT LEAST NOT THE *WHOLE* TRUTH. IT MUST HAVE BEEN ABOUT THAT *MORNING*, ABOUT THOSE CLOTHES, THE FOOD.
I HAD TO *WONDER* –

Ho! WIZARDS!
Wh – ?

Ain't yer land, wizards.
Oh!
Good day, my friends. Good day!
I am Dunstan, son of Dourlain, apprentice trade-wizard late of the great city of Keneil.
I bid you fair greeting, and come without –
Kid, what...?
IT WAS WHAT MY FATHER HAD TAUGHT ME.
BE CALM, WEAR A FRIENDLY FACE, AND SHOW THAT YOU THREATEN NO ONE. OF ANY TEN STRANGERS, FULLY EIGHT WILL DO THE SAME. BUT –

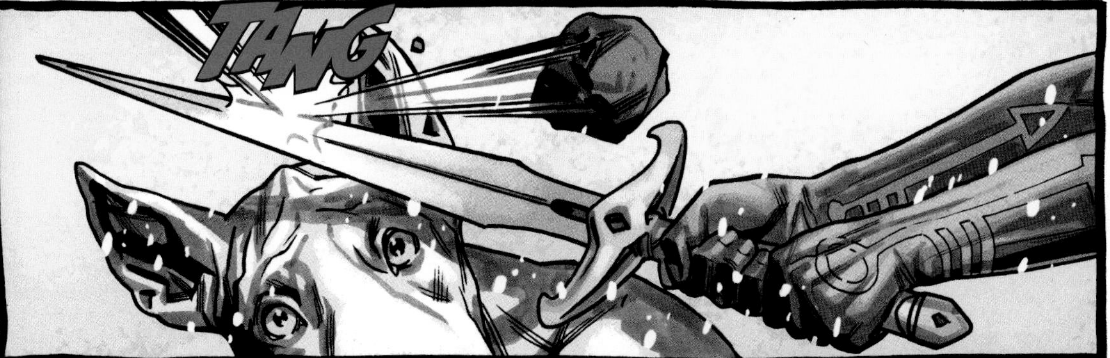

Dusty, behind me!

WIZARDS!

We're not...

Fakkin' wizards –

OUAAAHHH!

– IT'S THE *OTHER* TWO OF TEN, MY FATHER SAID, THAT A WISE MAN IS *WARY* OF.

MOST OF THEM WENT FOR *LEAROYD*, SINCE HE WAS OBVIOUSLY THE MORE ABLE WARRIOR.

I CONJURED *EBLENNIN'S FIRST PYROTIC*, AND TRIED TO FIGURE OUT WHO TO *USE* IT ON –

Back, Dusty! For fuck's sake, get the fuck –
-uhh!

Ye'll fakkin' pay, wizard!
All of ye! All yer foul –
Nnh!

Hff!
Fuh!
HNHH!

OUULLH!
Goddamn fuckin shitface assholes –

WRAK

KRAK

I don't know what this is about –
– an' I don't want to have to *kill* all you smelly-ass shitbrains if there's no reason to –
– but I *will* if you don't –

JACKIE!
HRRRR...
I WAS DAZED — COULDN'T MAKE SENSE OF IT ALL —
AND LEAROYD —
Oh, shit.
H-UHH!
Ahp —
AND —

HNHH!
Nnh
Hh
h
ff
Dusty! *Grab* something!
I c-c–
– AND I DIDN'T THINK MUCH FOR A *WHILE* AFTER THAT.

WHEN I *DID* START TO THINK AGAIN, I REALIZED LEAROYD PROBABLY COULD HAVE *AVOIDED* THAT BIG GOAT — JACKIE —

— IF HE HADN'T BEEN SHIELDING *ME.*

THEN THERE WAS *LIGHT* — HARSH LIGHT — IT HURT —

Are you...are you two *wizards*, then? Like, wi' the magic spells an' all?

That kinda wizards? 'Cause if y'are, we could rilly *use* a wizard or two abaht now...

Three

Lemme see. Lemme see!
We was here f —
Ooo. What's him?
We was figurin' on that, 'fore we was innerRUPted.
Emmer! Don't!
Poli says he's a bear, but I says where's his pelt an' Poli says he got sheared an' I says bears don't get sheared an' anyhow he don't look like —
I can talk, Lim. Din't say he was a bear either, said mebbe.
Maybe he's a nape, like inna jungles. I seen pictures.
Napes got hair too, an' don't get sheared neither.
Panther?
Panthers is like poomers an' mountain lines. He look like some cat, wi' those ears?
He's a manatee.
A what?
Manatee. Got no wool, no fur, no lizardy scales. 'S a... a sea creature, like.
Sea creature? In Erries?

An Among the Trees

by
Aliz Bougon

Illustrated by
DiPremma Todash

The town of Erries was unremarkable. And even if it weren't, there were few to remark on it.

Even the name was ordinary. Sheeptowns dotted hills and plains, wherever there was water for a mill and land not quite fertile enough for other tribes to take it from them. And often, they were named Erries. Or Arris, Urry, Harriz or any of a dozen variations.

It was a sheeptown name, and they liked it that way.

The rest was no different. Buildings made of local wood, of daub-and-wattle walls, roofed with thatch and snug within. A few important buildings of stone—the village hall, the brewery, the main granary, the mill. Visitors could be excused for confusing it with other sheeptowns.

Not that many visited to be confused. More than a small span of miles from Erries, few even knew it existed, aside from the occasional peddler trading metal goods and glass for thick, soft, Erries-made blankets, wool thread or a few barrels of the sweet malty ale they brewed. But when did a peddler let others know where his goods came from?

And the seasons turned and life changed little. And like all sheepclans, those of Erries were content. They had their ways, and their ways were fine.

Or so it went, until it went so no longer. But there were visitors, then...

Y'mean *mermaids.*

An' there ain't no such thing, parson says.

Like he'd know. When's *he* ever see'd a sea?

When has *you?*

WHEN WE *WOKE* AGAIN, IT WAS COOL BUT NOT COLD, DARK BUT FOR CANDLELIGHT. I REMEMBERED THE SHEEP WHO *FOUND* US, BUT NOTHING AFTER.

I MUST HAVE *PASSED OUT* AGAIN. AND LEAROYD –

Learoyd. He's Dusty.
And okay, I'll bite. Just exactly why do you need a wizard so bad?
Well, it's th' mountain, y'see.
There's summat going on. Summat there. An' we fear that...that we angered it somehow...

"THERE WAS...A GREAT SHAKIN', SCANT WEEKS BACK. AN' STRANGE LIGHTS IN THE EAST. AN' THEN ONLY DAYS LATER...
"...TH' MOUNTAIN, IT SEEMED TO RESPOND. LIGHTS IN THE NIGHT SKY, STRANGE, THREATENIN' LIGHTS...

"...AN' THEN THE SICKNESS COME, STRIKIN' OUR BEASTS OF BURDEN, OUR OLD AN' INFIRM...

...e'en our childern!
See! See how bad it is!

Gods of Health and Welfare!
So many!

Aye. Too many.
So y'see why we need wizardly help. Who else could stop this? Who else could save our lambs?

Well, the thing is, we're really not —
...not supposed to talk about that, Dusty.
Wh—?
Confidential business, Clan Chief Tavisher. You understand.

O' course, o' course!
I wouldn't mean t' pry into yer business, not at all!
But please, if ye're feelin' up to it —

— let me show ye about our town. Let me show you Erries.
A sheeptown? Yeah, that'd —
You brought us to safety, clan chief. You bound our wounds. We'd be pleased to see your town.
IT WAS FASCINATING. IN MANY WAYS, IT WAS LIKE ONE OF OUR MARKET SQUARES, IN THE CITIES ABOVE, BUT MUCH SMALLER, QUIETER.
I HAD NEVER SEEN UNGROUND GRAIN BEFORE. NEVER THOUGHT ABOUT IT BEING GROWN.
AND HERE I WAS, SEEING IT WITH MY OWN EYES.
AND THERE WAS SO MUCH TO SEE —
Nice town.
Aye, ordinarily. We're quite proud o' Erries, we are.
If...if it's not too presumptuous — when we found you, how did you come to — ?
...
There were goats.

Ah, aye. They're havin' troubles, too.
Normally, we'd be defending th' town against raids on our storehouses an' granaries. But th' mountain plagues them too, this season.
Here, here, take a look — a *fine* wool crop, or I'm no judge.
Ah, yes. Looks...excellent. But back to the goats. They seem to think, whatever these troubles are...
...they're being caused by wizards.

Well, o' course. No offense to ye, or to yer friend, o' course. Our runners tracked ye back eastward, so we know it warn't you...
...but who else would be doin' it? The gods?
I...suppose.
Wool? That's how they make wool?

You tell him it's a spot of housekeeping up in the hills, nothing more. And leave it at that — it'll just drive him sideways, won't it?
"A spot of housekeeping..."
Hm?
Nothing, nothing. It's a good question.

Dusty. Where are the Ramblelands? Anywhere near here?
What? No. Far, far south, in the shadow of the Dragonspine Range. I wouldn't think anyone here would even have *heard* of them.
Are you... remembering...?
No, no, just something I heard.

AND THEN HE GOT VERY *THOUGHTFUL* –
And this is your town mill? Tidy bit of work – you must be proud.
Oh, yes, yes. In my father's time, we ground the grain by hand. Backbreakin' work, I c'n tell ye.
We hired a sheenist from the west. Expensive, to be sure...
...but we've almost recovered from the expense of it. Three good seasons, no more, an' we'll be in profit.

Meanwhile, we mill more grain – an' finer grain – than any sheep-town in th' mountains.
I'm sure you do, a fine mill like that.

And speaking of grain, I hate to impose, but we last ate yesterday. Would your hospitality extend to a taste of your wares?
Ha! Well said, sir.
– AND I NOTICED, HIS SPEECH HAD CHANGED –

Ye're uncommonly polite for a wiza– I mean, a visitor.
I think we c'n do a bit better'n a taste, my friends. If y'would, sirs...

...we'd be delighted to have ye *dine* with us!
Will ye do us the honor?

RRAH! HURRAH
HE WIZARDS!
RRAH! HURRA
IT WAS QUITE A FEAST.

THERE WERE *CAKES*, VEGETABLES, BREADS, *FRUIT* IN PASTRY –
THEY EVEN ROASTED ONE OF THEIR YOUNG *FIELD DRAGONS* FOR US, EVEN THOUGH THEY DID NOT EAT *MEAT*.
IT WAS NOT COOKED *WELL*, BUT IT WAS A VERY NICE GESTURE.

Hihih!
AS FOR THE *REST* –
Well.

Food, free beer...
...I think I like this town!
I don't know...

MY FATHER *TALKED* OF THESE MOUNTAIN COMMUNITIES. NEVER MUCH, BUT SOME.
HE SAID THE FOLK HERE WERE *SIMPLE*.
INCAPABLE OF MORE THAN LIVES OF *LABOR*, AND UNCOMPREHENDING THAT THERE COULD BE ANYTHING *MORE*.

BUT THIS – IT WAS NOT WHAT I *EXPECTED*.
THEY HAD *COMMUNITY*, AND PRIDE, AND *HOPE*, AND LOVE.
ASIDE FROM THE SHADOW OF THE TROUBLE THEY FACED, THEY SEEMED *HAPPY*.

AND THEY HAD GREAT *FAITH* IN US. TOO *MUCH* FAITH –
Uh... magister wizard, sir?
W-we wannit to ask.

Yeah?
A-are ye a mermaider, sir? Or a *nape?* Or Poli says...
What *is* you, sir?

Heh. I'm a *sergeant,* kid. From what I hear, there haven't been any in this area for a long, long time. Eh, Dusty?
Hnh!

Hee! He think I'm a *goat!* Izzy blind?
Kid! He said *kid!*
Excuse me. Ahem.
We'd like to thank you for this, uh, sumptuous repast, folks.
And in return, my apprentice here can entertain you with a few simple...

Huh?

The mountain.
The mountain...
Well, that's...
...that's a hell of a *thing*, isn't it?
It is indeed.
And so ye see, sir, how badly we're in need of ye. Those lights, the sickness...
We'll offer whatever ye need. We're not a wealthy village...
...but anything we have, it's yers. *Anything.*
You're clearly a generous fellow, Clan Chief Tavisher. And you've caught our interest with this... fascinating situation.
As for compensation, we could —
We, uh, don't need your money.
What?
You're clearly under great enough strain already, and we wouldn't dream of adding to it.

Just some travel supplies. Food. Packs. Bedrolls and some cookware...
Yes! Yes, we c'n do that! O' course, o' course!
All you need! All you want!

And don't let your children — or any of the ill — drink water from the river, not 'til you hear from us.
No, no! Small beer from here on! An' thank you! Thank you!
I'll go prepare...
HE WENT, AND —

Ahh, thanks! You're too good to me, darlin'.
A pleasure, magister.
The water, kid?

Look around. Only the young and the very old drink water.
The others all drink ale, which was brewed before the sickness began. So if whatever's happening has tainted the water...
Huh. Not bad.
Sharp fuckin' thinking, kid!

HURRAH! HURRAH THE WIZARDS! HU RAH!
THE FEAST WENT ON 'TIL THE EARLY HOURS. IT WAS AS IF THEY THOUGHT WE'D ALREADY SOLVED THEIR TROUBLES.

AND THE NEXT *MORNING* –
What... what's he doin'?

He's...shearin' his *face*?
Can y'spin *wool* from that?
It's called shaving. It's a...thing sergeants do.
Hi! Magister Dog, sir!
Oh, aye. If ye say so, sir.
Nothing to worry about.

Y'r packs, sir. Everything ye asked for. Plus a dram o' my gran's blackberry liniment. For th' nights, y'unnerstan?
Ah –
An' this.

He left it in th' hospital, sir. Wouldn't want you to think we'd kyped it...
Um –
I ALMOST TOLD HIM TO *KEEP* IT. IT HAD TO BE *VALUABLE* –
– AND IT'D PAY THEM BACK FOR ALL THEY'D *GIVEN* US, IF WE *WEREN'T* ABLE TO HELP THEM.

BUT –

– I HAD QUESTIONS ABOUT IT *MYSELF.* AND WHAT IT *MEANT.* IT WASN'T ANY METAL I KNEW. MAYBE NOT ONE *ANY* OF THE TRIBES KNEW.
AND THEY PROBABLY WOULDN'T SELL IT *ANYWAY.* BUILD A *SHRINE* TO IT, MORE LIKE, TO REMEMBER THE DAY THE *WIZARDS* CAME.

AND SO WE LEFT *ERRIES.*
Hurrah!
Hurrah!
IT WAS A NICE LITTLE VILLAGE. A *HAPPY* VILLAGE, OR SO IT SEEMED, BEFORE THE LIGHTS IN THE SKY.
AND *WE* –

WE'D PROMISED TO *HELP THEM,* BUT –
H'ray!
H'rah!

Cheer up, kid, it ain't the end of the fuckin' world. I think.
Not that a little cash wouldn't have been welcome, Mister "We Don't Want Your Money"...
I just – I just feel like we lied to them. Letting them think we're wizards –

Ah, you're just too goddamn honest, Dusty. Besides, you are a wizard.
You called me an *apprentice!*
I'm barely a *beginner!* I know maybe ten or twelve spells, only a *handful* of them well!

That's a handful more than *they* do.
But what if — what if we can't help them?
Then they're no worse off than if we hadn't fallen into their back forty, right? We didn't beat out other applicants for the job.
Hell, you probably already paid 'em back with that tip about the water.

But — we —
I DIDN'T *UNDERSTAND.*
HE *WANTED* TO GO UP THE MOUNTAIN, I KNEW THAT.
Pick up the pace there, Dusty.
WE'D BE HEADED THERE EVEN IF THE SHEEP HADN'T GIVEN US A *THING.*
I JUST DIDN'T KNOW *WHY.* AND I DIDN'T KNOW —

h'ray!
WE WERE HEADED INTO *DANGER.* UNKNOWN, POTENTIALLY *DEADLY* DANGER.
AND HE SEEMED... *HAPPY.*

THE GREAT CHAMPION OF LEGEND – THE HERO WE'D THOUGHT HIM TO BE – WOULD HAVE SALLIED FORTH JUST BECAUSE IT WAS THE RIGHT THING TO DO.
BUT THIS CHAMPION –
I WAS LEARNING THAT LEGENDS WERE A POOR GUIDE. HE HAD REASONS FOR ALL HE DID. HIS OWN REASONS. WHETHER I UNDERSTOOD OR NOT –
Goats!
Huh?
What about the goats? They'll be –
Pff.
You let me worry about the goats, kid.
I'm all over that.
AND WE CRESTED A RISE, AND –
DID – WHATEVER IT WAS – STILL SHINE AND WRITHE IN THE SKY? EVEN DURING THE FULL LIGHT OF DAY?
DID IT GLINT AND CRACKLE, ALMOST TOO FAINTLY TO SEE? OR DID I IMAGINE IT?
I COULDN'T TELL.

Come on, kid. We're burnin' daylight.
THERE WAS SO MUCH I COULDN'T TELL.
SO MUCH –
Kaark.

Four

THE MOUNTAINS –
THE MOUNTAINS WERE –

The Bones of the Earth

by

RENCAR INTERRA

The mountains were old, the oldest known places in the Autumnlands. Not all mountains, it is true—there were young mountains, raw mountains, thrust up from below by chaos and the wars of the gods. But these mountains, and many others, were ancient. From before the Summerlands, before the Dawning Lands. They had been old even in the time of legends, and they had seen much.

They had seen cataclysm, fire, the ur-energies of creation sweeping over the hills and plains and valleys below, over rivers and seas. They had seen the world reshaped, time and again, and they watched, silent and undisturbed, protecting their secrets.

There were those who believed they were bones, their long ranges the spines of leviathans long dead, monsters that once roamed the earth—fought, devoured, bled and died. And those who said they were merely rock, but rock the gods had walked before they were gods. Rock they had huddled in for refuge from greater forces even than they.

Whatever they were, they had seen much. Endured much. And sheltered much. Many said they still did. Ancient things, powerful things. Sacred and demonic things. Those who braved their peaks had to be brave themselves, and those who sought their secrets at least a little foolish.

For those who returned from the peaks brought dark tales. And many never returned at all...

ILLUSTRATED BY **ROGAR**

THE MOUNTAINS HELD MUCH THAT WAS *UNKNOWN* TO ME, THOUGH I HAD LOOKED AT THEM FROM ABOVE ALL MY LIFE.
HIIIIIIIIIIIH – !
THE WIND, THE *DAMP*, THE UNENDING, WEARYING SLOPES. AND THE SHADOWED *FORESTS* THAT HID ONLY THE GODS KNEW WHAT –

LEAROYD HAD GONE TO GATHER *BREAKFAST*. I SAW TO THE WATER –
DUSTY! Hey!

What're you doing, kid?
The stream – look to your right!

Huh? It's just – GHAH!

THEY WERE – CHANGED, MUTATED, *MONSTROUS* –
What – what –

Wildlife and fisheries! They're –
The forest's full of shit like that. No animals fit to eat.
The water's fucking tainted, kid. It's not safe to drink – you're the one pointed that out in the first place.

Yes, but –

– I can clean it.
Well, fuck me running – it scans as pure. *Really* pure. Another handy-dandy magic spell?

It's *VanDahl's All-Purpose Purification.* We use it for – well, everything.
Cleaning clothes, preparing food, keeping injuries from festering...
It's how I kept your bandages clean, from your shoulder wound.
Huh.

I cleaned the water they had stored down in Erries, as well. The rainwater tanks were fine, but the river water...*euh.*
And you didn't think to tell me?
I wasn't all that good at it yet, back home. But I've been getting a lot of practice.
And I feel like I've been getting better and better at it, since we headed up the mountain. What I just did?
It'd have taken me an hour, a month ago.

Yeah?
You want my advice, kid...

...do it a *lot.*
Aw, hell, they're everywhere.

The closer we get to whatever's causing this, the nastier it's getting.
Purify the water, the food, the fucking ground we sleep on. Just purify the shit out of –

Kaark.
Avenger.
Kaark.
Oh, great.

Goddamn weird fucking crow-ass shitheads!
Kaark. Kaark. Liberator!
What the fuck *are* they, Dusty?

I...I don't know. I never saw anything like them. Never even heard of anything like them.
But what they're saying –
What they're saying is *shit.*
What kind of a world *is* this, anyway? You've got talking snake-people and ordinary snakes, you've got birds that wear clothes and those things.
You got frogs? *And* you got frog-wizards?
You didn't? Back in your time, you didn't have wise yumanbeins and simple, primitive yumanbeins?
Well, not the way you mean, anyway.
I don't think you want to hear about election years...

How strange a world it must have been. Yumanbeins but no unshaped ones?
Tell me...

...what did you eat? Learoyd?

Learoyd?
SUDDENLY, THERE WAS A *GREAT RUSTLING* IN THE UNDERBRUSH, AND –

Wizard. Wizard!
Oh, n-no – !

I'll kill ye, wizard! I'll –

WHUMPP

Hah! Motherfucking *goats!*
Told you I'd take care of them. Spotted this joker, made my way into the trees, and —

Oh, fuck. Did I touch any of that?
He's sick. Get the water, Learoyd, and a cloth.

It's definitely getting easier. I'm drawing more magic, more *hatsas* — some *much* more easily than before.
He tried to *kill* you, kid. Why are you fixing him up?

Because he's sick, Learoyd. Because he needs help.
Isn't that enough?

Yeah, I guess. Maybe.
And maybe he can fill us in a little more...

"...ON WHAT THE HELL'S *GOING ON* UP THERE..."

I — ah — Whoa. That's so strange...
What? What's strange?
It's the magic —
— it's really *strong!* It feels — feels different somehow, but —
I can *feel* it — his disease, his illness! And I'm not even calling on my crystal!
And I think I can —
What?
His sores are gone — his face — did you just super-clean him, or —
Uh?
Hanh?

Wah-
HEY!
Try t'take me on now, y'wizards! Ah'll klop ye left an' I'll klop ye right!
I'll klop ye so bad, ye —

Oh.
This were... you, weren't it?

Ye magicked me, eh? Fix me up, try'n'make me a slave?
Goats don' slave, wizards.

An' Dirty Aelbert o' the Hardhill Clan bows his horns t'no master — no lord, no sheep, no fackin wizard!
So y'think yer hard enough t'butt this head, you got another —

Ah —

A'right, a'right. I'll o'erlook it this time.
But the goats of Hardhill don' trust magic an' don' use it. So I'll warn ye not to try that again.
What? If he hadn't *healed* you, you little –
Shh, shh.

Your name's... Dirty Aelbert?
Well. Sometimes. Me mates call me Bertie, mostly.
But the nannies – ah, the nannies *like* it dirty, don't they? Ya-*hah!*
And, ah, what brings you up *here*, Bertie?

We got the *sickness* down below, somethin' fierce. The kids, the auldhorns, the fightin' bills...
I come up to find the Craglanders. They guard the oldest an' wisest of us, an' we need answers.
We...need answers *soon.*

There's a goatclan up here?
'Course there is!
The goatclans live *high!* The goatclans live *hard!* We're no sheeptown, to suckle up to –

...the fuck?

Earthquake. But no foreshocks, no minor temblors. What was –
Learoyd!
Learoyd, look –

Oh, shit.
Oceans an' Atmospheres, daughters o' Commerce! Spare me from yer –
No time, no time – get down! Down in a ditch! In anything! Just get –

Okay, kid, what the fuck was *that* trick? Not that I'm not glad of it, but –
The shield-spells we use in the Cities Above, to keep them from being scoured clean by the fierce winds.
I never *could* master them before, but –
Oh, Great Idente Above All. I know what this *is!*

It's the magic!
It's *hatsas* – magic! All *around!* All we could *want!* Even *I* can use it – a mere beginner! It's raw – different – *really* different, but –
Huh?

This is what we've been *looking for!* You're the *Great Champion!* You were brought here to *restore magic*, to *save the world!*
Here it *is!* The magic! This is what you're *here for!*

Wait. He's th' Great *what?*
All we have to do is find the *source!* Find it and *unleash* it across –
Kid –

Take *cover!*

What in the name of the Wildlife Children – ?
They were fleeing those winds. Fleeing that "source" you're all charged up about. It's the source of the toxins, too, the mutation.
This isn't going to be as easy as you think.
Hey-hey!

More comin'!
But you'll not get *me*, ye foul things! Ye'll not get *Dirty Aelbert* o' the *Hardhill Clan!*
Too *swift!* Too *nimble!* Hah! Ya-*hey!*

Bertie. Dirty Aelbert. You were almost *one* of them, you know that? A day or two more, and –
Who cares, dog? I'm hale! I'm *hearty!* An' these stinkin', oozy beasties, they can't get –

– ARHHH!
SPLOWW

EUHH!
Scrub me clean again, wizard! Scrub me clean!

Huh. Those dino — field dragons are domesticated, aren't they? And I'd swear that one had a bridle around its neck.
Goat-boy. How far off is this clan of yours?

It's Aelbert ta you, hornless. An' the Craglanders aren't far.
They're just over that —

WHOOMTHOOM

KRAKKKK KRAMMM

HRRRRR...

wa-hey?

Five

Jesus shit!
Scatter!

"CURSED THING! Your reign of terror ends here!" The steely-eyed hero of legend shifted his grip on his sword hilt and commanded his followers. "I've slain worse than this before—and so can you! We need only co-ordinate our attacks! Aelbert, you get behind it, slash its hindleg tendons when you get a chance! I'll draw its attention! Dunstan, hit it with a Cone of Confusion, then VanDahl's Soothing Sleep!"

"I-I'll try," the faithful pup-wizard quavered.

But Aelbert of the Hardhill Clan was not so easily rallied.

"Are ye mad, Great One?" the scrappy young goat-warrior gasped. "Meanin' no offense, but yon

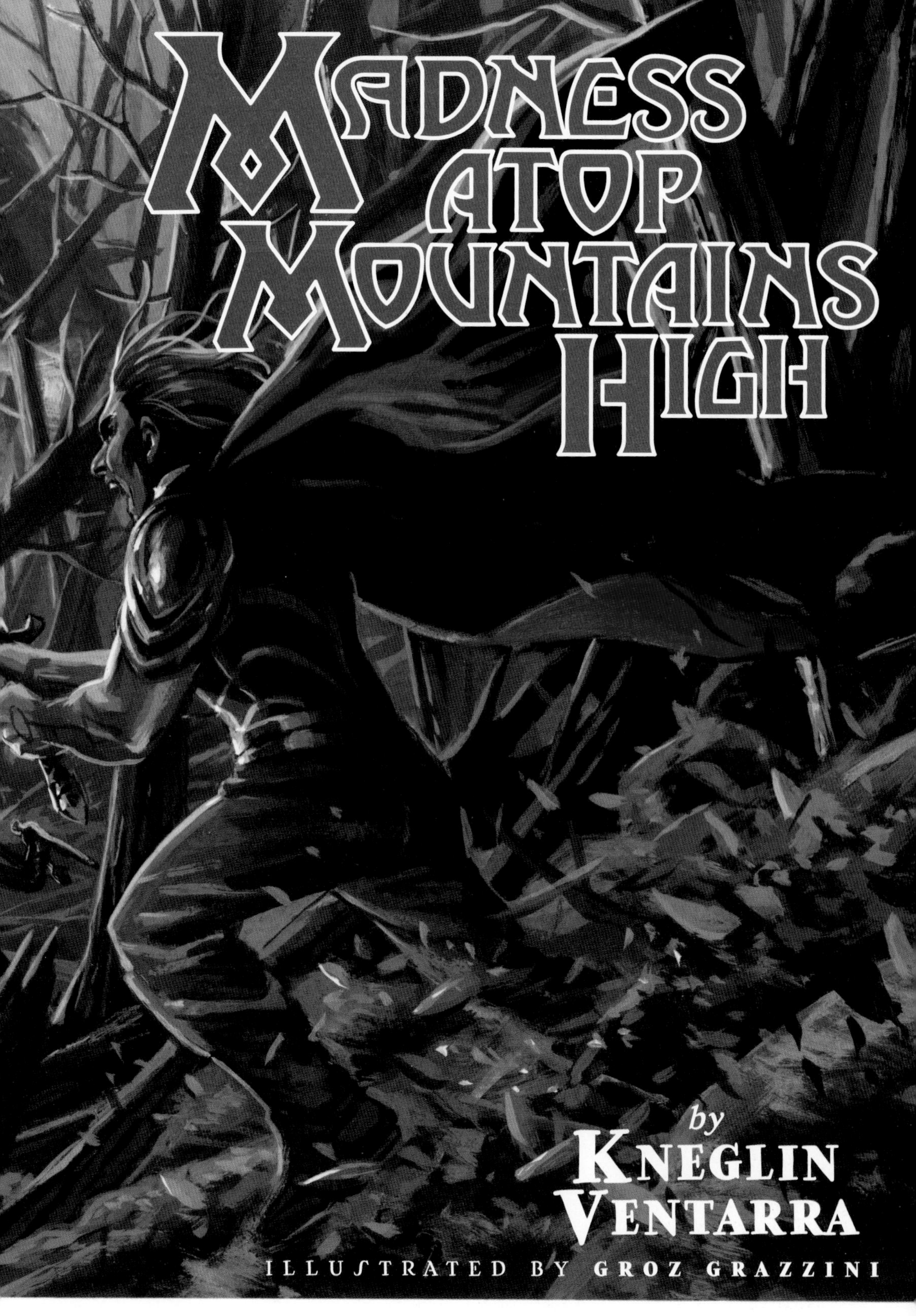

thing's got eyes in th' back of its heid! Godchilders o' Science an' Industry, it's got *heids* in th' back o' its heid! An' god o' Defense save me, but I think I *know* some of 'em!"

And young Bertie was right. For the creature before them was all that was left of the Craglanders, the peak-dwelling goatclan he'd come to find. Poisoned by toxic magic, mutated by forces that had slumbered for centuries, they had merged, in their maddened state—with one another and stricken lower beasts as well—and fused into a single entity, its dim, chaotic mind raging with pain and anger, lashing out at anything in its path.

But the Great Champion and his disciples were doughty and unafraid...

Fuck! Fuck fuck fuck fuck fuck!
I'm not fucking trained for fucking giant mutant goats!

I'm tellin' ye, thing, ye're lettin' 'em go!
Ye're lettin' the Craglanders go, an' right now —

RAKK
— or I ain't Dirty Aelbert o' the —

AW!
Leggo o' that! That's mine!

THERE WASN'T ANYTHING THEY COULD DO. NOT AGAINST SOMETHING LIKE THAT.
BUT I —

– I FELT LIKE I HAD ACCESS TO ALL THE MAGIC IN THE WORLD. IT WAS IN THE AIR, IN THE EARTH, ALL AROUND. IT WAS IN EVERYTHING –
– AND IF I COULD JUST CHANNEL IT, USE IT –
I-I'll take care of it. I'll hit it s-so hard...
Dusty! No! Get back, get to –
GRAR AA
– the fuck?!
Get the fuck away from me with that shit!
Dusty! Listen to me! You can't –
I DIDN'T LISTEN. I COULD FEEL IT, THE HATSAS. ALL THIS POWER, GATHERING AROUND ME, FLOWING INTO ME –

WAPP
Ach! Dusty!

UHHHH!

Not *him*! Look at *me*, you shitgoat! At *me*!
I COULDN'T *SEE* STRAIGHT –
– BUT I COULD SEE *MORE* –

I COULD SEE *WITHIN* IT –
DEEP WITHIN –

THE *DISEASE* AT ITS HEART – I COULD SEE IT, *FEEL* IT –
AND I WONDERED – WAS THIS WHAT IT WAS LIKE FOR *REAL* WIZARDS? COULD THEY SEE LIKE THIS ALL THE *TIME?*

Can feel it...
Un... unclean...
I can... can...

I *CLEANED* IT.

VANDAHL'S ALL-PURPOSE PURIFICATION. I'D NEVER *TRIED* IT ON THAT KIND OF SCALE, BUT I FELT LIKE – LIKE I COULD DO *ANYTHING* –

I MUST HAVE *PASSED OUT*, THOUGH NOT FOR LONG. BUT WHEN I *AWOKE* –
Oh.
Oh, no...
THEY WERE ALL DEAD. OR *NEARLY* DEAD.
THOSE THAT STILL LIVED – THEY WOULDN'T LIVE *LONG*.
AND I –
I... did all this.
I k-killed them...
An' there's Angus, and yon's Wise Harfa...Tricky Lem, Gray Cobb...
Wasn't you that did this, Dusty. This was done *to* them.
You just set 'em free. Let 'em die clean.

I'm...I'm sorry...
IT WASN'T LIKE I *THOUGHT* IT WOULD BE. IT DIDN'T FEEL *GOOD.*
DIDN'T FEEL LIKE I'D TRIUMPHED. LIKE I'D WON *ANYTHING.*

You got nothin' t'be sorry abaht, wizard.
They were Craglanders. They lived free, they lived hard, and they bowed horns to no...

To no...

I'm comin' wi' you.
I came fer answers from the greybeards o' the crags. I'm not gettin' 'em. But I'll *have* answers. I'll have answers from *someone.*
An' they'll answer for *all* of this.

AND SO WE WERE *THREE.*
That's it ahead. The peak the lights come from at night.

That cleansing spell, Dusty. Cast it on all of us. Cast it a lot.
I have been. I've got it going continuously, sort of.
I didn't even know that was possible, but I'm –

Good.
I COULD STILL *FEEL* IT, ALL AROUND US.
THE MAGIC, BOTH THE *HATSAS* I'D KNOWN ALL MY LIFE, AND THE WARPED, *UNCLEAN* MAGIC.
BUT IT DIDN'T FEEL EVIL. IT JUST FELT... *DIFFERENT.* RAW, CRUDE. *UNSHAPED.*

AND I COULD *FEEL* –
Learoyd! We're close! The source of it all, it's –

Huh.

Dusty. Is this familiar? Anything like this in your cities, your temples?
Some...some of the symbols on the facade are like those of the Children of Feniz, Goddess of Energy, but...not fully...

The rockfall was recent, but before it – this rock face was sealed for tens of thousands of years. Maybe more.
Whatever this place is, it's *old.*
I FELT MAGIC – *RAW MAGIC,* IF THAT'S WHAT IT WAS – MAKING MY *HEART* BEAT FASTER, MY *HAIR* STAND UP –
AND *SOUNDS,* JUST AHEAD –

They're...they're like you...!
Not like me, kid. Not hardly.
Whoah.
Look at th' dugs on them nannies...!

If you are not a master, you must be destroyed.

Hey, now. There's no need for that, ma'am.

We just want to ask a few questions about –

WHRACKK

Well, shit.

Codeword, codeword...
Feniz?
Incorrect.

Shit, shit, shit.
Dusty! *Distract* her!
What?

Excuse me! What — could you tell us what you are? What is a Galatean?
We are the Galateans.
If you do not give the codeword, you must be destroyed.

Come *on*, you fucking shitpile, get online! If there's any data on...
Ah! Galatea... and Leucippus, Galatea sea nymph, Galatea *statue!* Myth of sculptor who fell in love with his own...

Ch-chisel! Beauty! S-statue! Uh –
ƐhkkƐ Honkers! Teats! ƐchhƐ M-milkbags!
No.

Pygmalion!
No.
Shit. Paphos! Ovid! Aphrodite!
No.

What the *hell*, then?
Henry Higgins?

Codeword accepted.
Welcome back, master.
Ɛk-uhh!Ɛ

We are...in some disarray, masters. But we may offer hospitality and comfort.
You must have traveled far. Would you like a meal?
Uh... yes?

Don't look at me, I don't know shit about ancient literature.
Something about a bet, and maybe some dancing...
IT FELT — LIKE A DREAM.
LIKE NOTHING MADE SENSE, BUT IT WOULD IF WE COULD ONLY GRASP IT. STILL, THE INTERIOR OF THE MOUNTAIN WAS COOL, THE AIR FRESH —
— AND WITHIN MINUTES, WE CAME TO —
We sent the request ahead to those of us within.
Our apologies. We had to synthesize the food, as our stores were no longer usable due to partial power failure. I hope it will suffice.
And we can, at least...

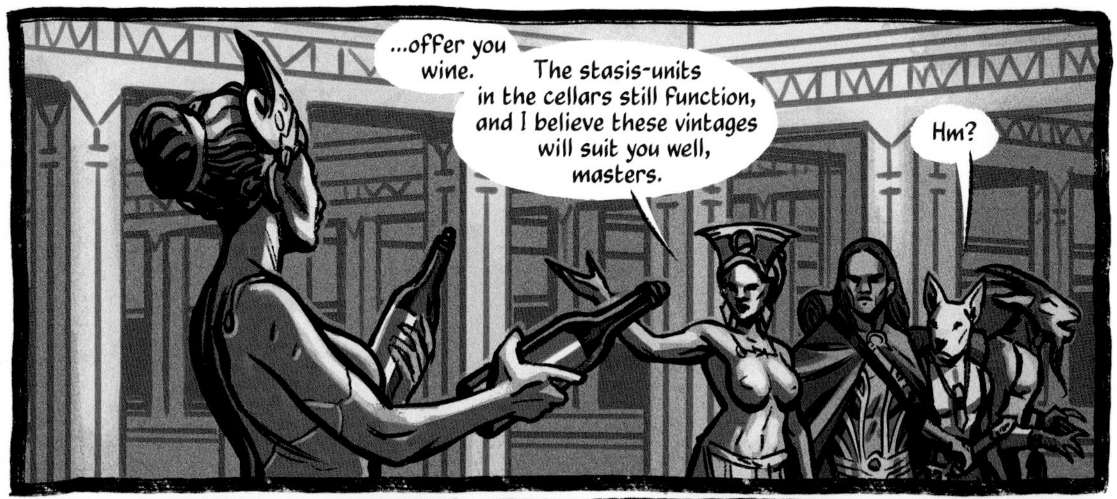
...offer you wine.
The stasis-units in the cellars still function, and I believe these vintages will suit you well, masters.
Hm?

This is...they created this food? Is it safe?
It...scans okay. But I wouldn't want to risk it without further...

Aw, this is *great!*
CHOFF CHOFF
Y'gotta try this — *whate'er* kinda bird it is, it's delicious! Th'bread don't compare t' sheepbread, but I've had worse!
Grab a chair an' slosh out some o' that firewater, willya?

What I wanna know *mmf mff*
What *I* wanna know —

D'those stone wrappins come off, eh? Are ye all-stone, or are ye *equipped*, hey?
We are.
Do you desire to lie with us, Master Goat?

Wah-
HEY!
THERE WAS SOMETHING THAT FELT...WRONG ABOUT THIS PLACE. THESE WOMEN. AND I COULD SEE THAT LEAROYD FELT THE SAME.

BUT THE GALATEANS DID NOT FEEL LIKE A THREAT, NOT SINCE THEY HAD ACCEPTED US –
The furnishings in the pillow rooms are long rotted away. But we are creating new ones as we speak. We may attend you there soon.
Please, masters, relax yourselves. Eat and drink.
That...that won't be necessary.
Hey!
The food is excellent, and we thank you.

But...may we ask a question?
We exist to serve. Of course you may.
Then...

You've been sealed up here for a long time. I'd like to hear about that. But first, your temple...it only recently opened up again.
What happened to bring that about?

I cannot say if it was intentional.
The ground shook. There was a surge of energy, not entirely physical. It interfered with our stasis fields, allowed rock to fall.
Sunlight triggered reactivation thirty-four days ago.

When Keneil fell! It wasn't just impact — the levitation spells, the shield spells, they all ruptured, city-wide!
The effects — they could have reached this far —

A city... fell?
We have no referent for this. Cities do not fall, unless in metaphor. And this region...it is now inhabited?
Why did you poison the water?

Poison? Your water is pure, masters. Safe and healthy to tolerances of —
No, not here.
Outside, the streams, the water flowing from the mountain.

I...cannot say. We have done only our duty, as we were ordered.
Only our duty.
BUT SHE HESITATED. WAS SHE *CONFUSED?* OR WAS SHE TRYING TO DECEIVE US? I COULDN'T *TELL* —

Your duty. Your orders.
Please, tell me about that. Who were your first masters? Why did they create you? What is your purpose, or what was it when —

My apologies, masters. We are not here to ask questions of you, but to serve. To obey.
And we can communicate *silently,* when we wish.
I am sorry. I abase myself.
No, it's fine. You have a question? Ask away.

I thank you. In that case, I will ask for her.
You are our masters. We exist to obey. But time — it has been such a long time. Such a very long time. Please, masters —
— MAY WE DIE?

Six

"WHEN WE WERE INITIATED – GIVEN FORM – MUCH OF EARTH WAS UNINHABITABLE.
"THE PLAINS, THESE HILLS, ALL WAS BLANKETED IN RAW, SEETHING ENERGY. ALL BUT THE HIGHEST PEAKS.
"BUT EARTH WAS NOT LIFELESS –"
We're approaching – approaching –
Goddammit, hold it together – !

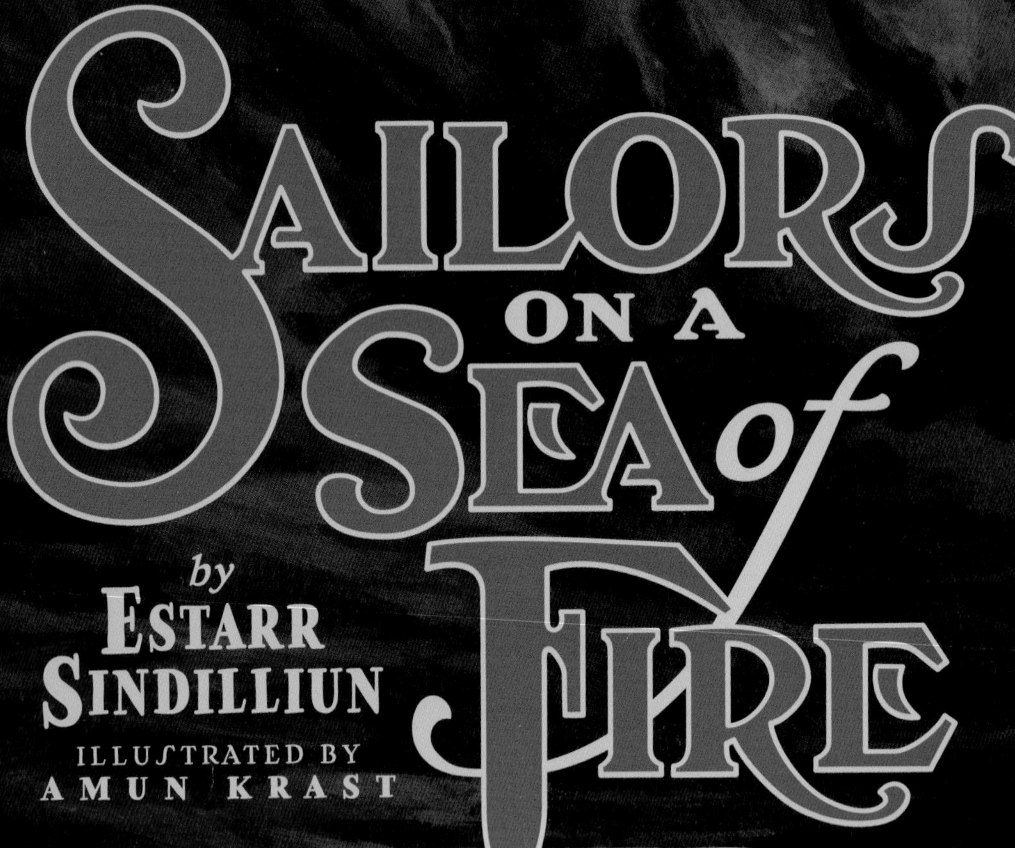

Sailors on a Sea of Fire

by **Estarr Sindilliun**

Illustrated by Amun Krast

They came across the burning oceans from lands unknown and unheralded. They came after the end of all, to begin anew.

They did not curse, and they did not waver. Though their coracle was tiny, and instant death heaved and swelled around them, they had great purpose, and their purpose gave them calm. Calm, and a quiet intent.

They did not thirst, nor did they hunger, though their ship's biscuit was long since eaten and their water drained, and there'd been scant rations of each even when they set out. But they had mighty spells protecting them. From fire, starvation, all manner of cruel fate.

And so they sailed, in their fragile craft, tossed and spun by burning waves. And they grew weak and faint, their flesh shriveling on their bones, their throats parched and swollen with need. But they did not pause. They did not cry out. They did not sleep.

"We forge on," they whispered, low and sand-voiced. "For we have mighty magicks to do, a world to shape. We forge on. Do you see it? Do you see it yet?" Dull-eyed, they peered forward, in hope of a horizon.

And then one day, the cry came. "Land! Land ho!"

It was not loud, for the lookout had lost all strength. But all heard her, with their hearts if not their ears.

And there it was, jutting above the flames...

"THEY CAME, THE MASTERS, TO THIS *VERY PEAK.*
"THEY CAME AND BUILT *GREAT MACHINES* –

"– AND THEN GATHERED *RAW ENERGY* AND *MOLTEN STONE,* AND SHAPED IT –"
Got it – got it –
Constructing now –

How's this?
Functional, but really? You want to watch *that* lumbering around?

Okay, okay. We can make 'em look like whatever we want, so –
Children's toys? Did you ever grow up?
Here, give me that –

Ah! Now we're talking! Hm? *Hm?*
Pierson, you have a one-track mind.
What? It's *classical!*

"THE MASTER MADE US ALL, AND SET US TO OUR TASKS.
"TO GATHER THE SEETHING ENERGIES, TO CONVERT AND CLEAN THEM –

"AND TO RELEASE THEM INTO THE ATMOSPHERE –

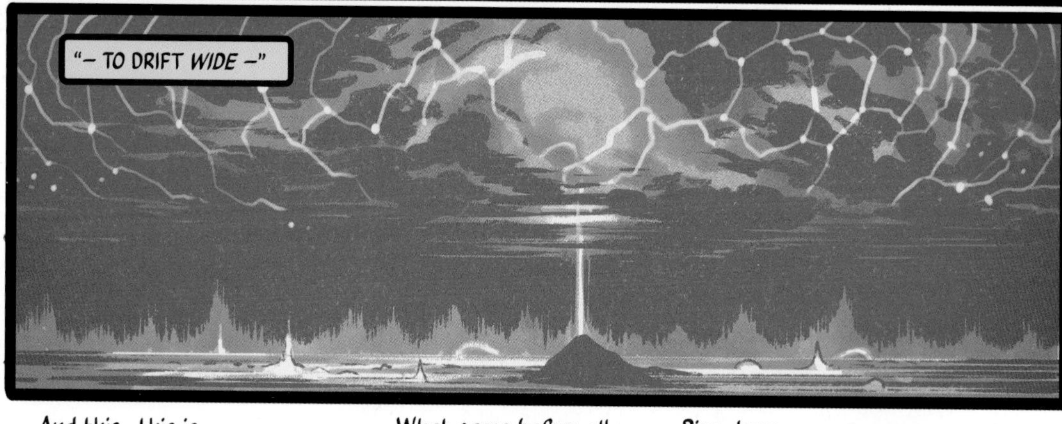
"– TO DRIFT WIDE –"

And this...this is hatsas? Magic? You spread it across the world? And the master, is he one of the gods?
What came before all these...energies? What caused them?
Pipe down, Dusty. Don't interrupt.

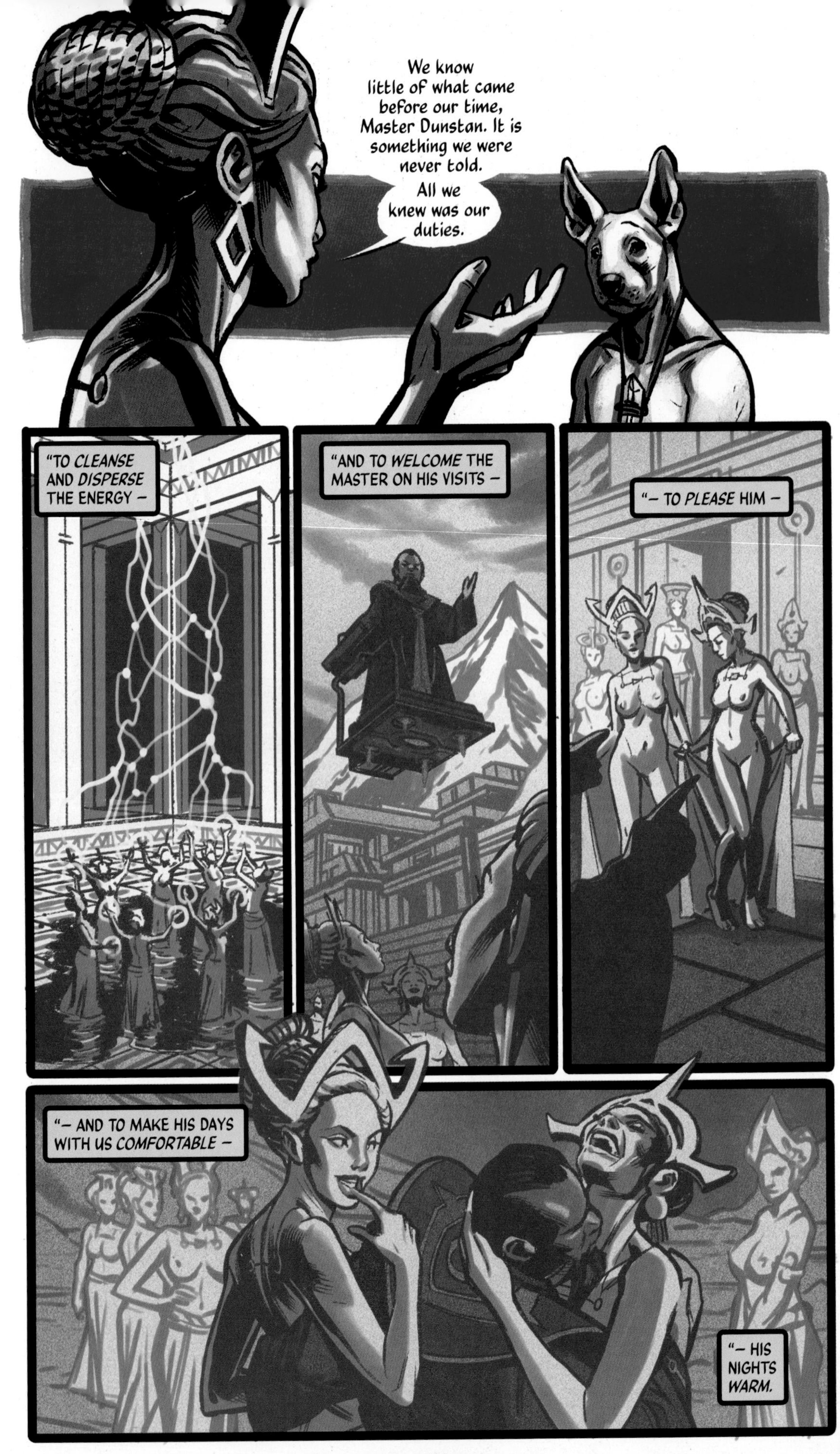
We know little of what came before our time, Master Dunstan. It is something we were never told.
All we knew was our duties.
"TO CLEANSE AND DISPERSE THE ENERGY –
"AND TO WELCOME THE MASTER ON HIS VISITS –
"– TO PLEASE HIM –
"– AND TO MAKE HIS DAYS WITH US COMFORTABLE –
"– HIS NIGHTS WARM.

"USUALLY, HE CAME ALONE.
"AT TIMES, HE BROUGHT OTHER MASTERS WITH HIM, AND WE SAW TO THEIR NEEDS TOO."
And...what did you Galateans think about that?
All this "pleasing" of the master and his friends?
We...
We do not...we did not think about such things.
We were built to perform our tasks. I suppose, if we had any reaction, it was to feel satisfaction at performing them well.
At fulfilling our duties as we were meant to.

"BUT OVER THE CENTURIES, THE MASTER WAS REPLACED BY *OTHER* MASTERS, AND THEY CAME LESS *FREQUENTLY.*

"FOR A LONG, LONG TIME, THEY DID NOT COME *AT ALL.*

"AND AS THE ENERGIES WERE CLEANSED, THE LAND BECAME *FERTILE* AGAIN. AND WE...

"THE MASTER HAD EQUIPPED THIS FACILITY WITH *LITERATURE,* WITH ART. FOR HIS PLEASURE DURING HIS VISITS.

"IN OUR EXTENDED PERIODS OF INACTIVITY, WE *READ,* AND LISTENED, AND *LOOKED.*

"AND WE *DISCUSSED* WHAT WE HAD READ. TRIED TO MAKE SENSE OF THESE *IMAGES,* THESE SOUNDS, THESE TALES OF GODS AND MEN, OF *LOVE...*

"...OF THE RISE AND FALL OF *NATIONS* AND THE YEARNINGS OF THEIR *PEOPLES.*

"IN TIME, A MASTER CAME ONCE AGAIN.
"WE BOWED TO HIM, AND OFFERED HIM WHAT PLEASURES HE MIGHT DESIRE –

"– BUT HE WAS NOT THERE FOR PLEASURE. OR TO ASSIGN US NEW TASKS.

"HE HAD COME TO END OUR LONG WORK.
"HE SAW US TO THE STORAGE RACKS. AND HE CLOSED DOWN THE FACILITY, SEALING IT OFF FROM THE WORLD OUTSIDE.

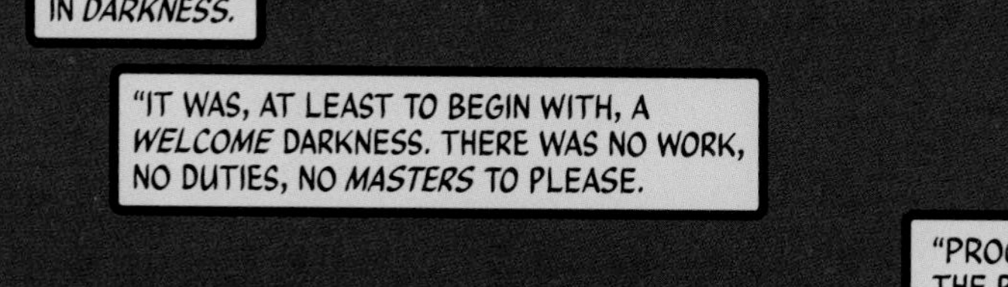
"WE EXISTED IN DARKNESS.
"IT WAS, AT LEAST TO BEGIN WITH, A WELCOME DARKNESS. THERE WAS NO WORK, NO DUTIES, NO MASTERS TO PLEASE.
"PROCESSES ABATED. WE MAINTAINED THE BAREST OF SLOWTIME. AND WE LET OUR MINDS DRIFT, THINKING, MUSING. TURNING OVER WHAT WE HAD LEARNED.

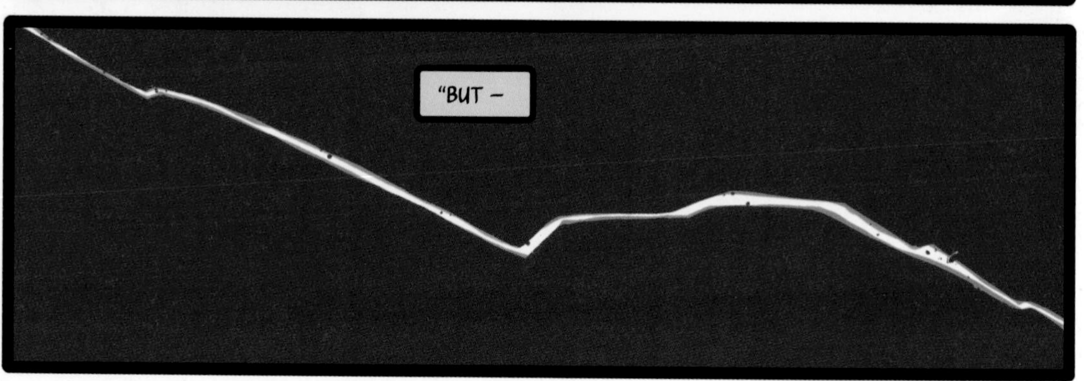
"BUT –

"IT WAS, AS I HAVE DESCRIBED, A GREAT SHOCK IN THE EARTH. IT ALLOWED LIGHT WITHIN THE FACILITY, BRINGING US BACK TO ACTIVE TIME.
"AND MORE –

"A STORAGE TANK WAS CRACKED. ENERGY WAS LEAKING.
"CLEARLY, WE HAD DUTIES ONCE MORE.

"WE GATHERED THE SPILLING ENERGY –
"– PURIFIED IT, RELEASED IT –"

Th' lights at night! In th' sky!
Sure, that makes sense. That was you, sending the cleansed energies into the upper atmosphere.
Yes. But there was more.

"WE HAD AGED, GROWN WORN AND CRACKED, AND OUR BODIES COULD WITHSTAND ONLY SO MUCH REPAIR. MOST OF US DID WHAT WE COULD.
"BUT SOME... DEFIED THEIR PURPOSE –
"– AND CHOSE FOR THEMSELVES.

"THEY *REMOVED* THEMSELVES FROM THE FACILITY, TO *EMPTY PLACES.* AND THEY..."

The explosions. That covers that, too.
And let me guess...

You're powered by the raw form of the energy, the toxic form.
So when some of you suicided, that let it out. That's what got in the water. Poisoned the people of Erries, and --
An' killed th' Craglanders. The *elders.* Turned 'em inta monsters an'...

I am...
...sorry about that, Master Aelbert. It was not authorized behavior.
And we did not know it would have such effects. Did not know the region was even inhabited.
Didn't *know!*

But that brings us back to our dilemma.
We are old. Faulty. Unneeded. We do not wish to be slaves, and we have no other purpose.
So I ask again. May we, after all these centuries, finally die? May we rest?

Uh...look, it shouldn't be up to...
The thing is, your energy's still toxic, right? Still a threat to others?

That does not need to be an issue.
The toxic events you describe were caused by uncontrolled disposals. There are other methods. Safer ones.
We could convert each Galatean's energy safely, dissipate it fully.
And then the last to remain could house herself in the tanks, leach out...

That's not — this may not be the best —
There may be other options. Better options. You read all those books, learned about struggle and yearning and love...
They could aid in our quest! Rebuild the world's stores of magic!
Right?
That's not... look, let me *think* about this, okay?

Of course.
In the meantime, since you've said you will not be using the pillow rooms, bedchambers have been prepared for each of you.

If you would...?

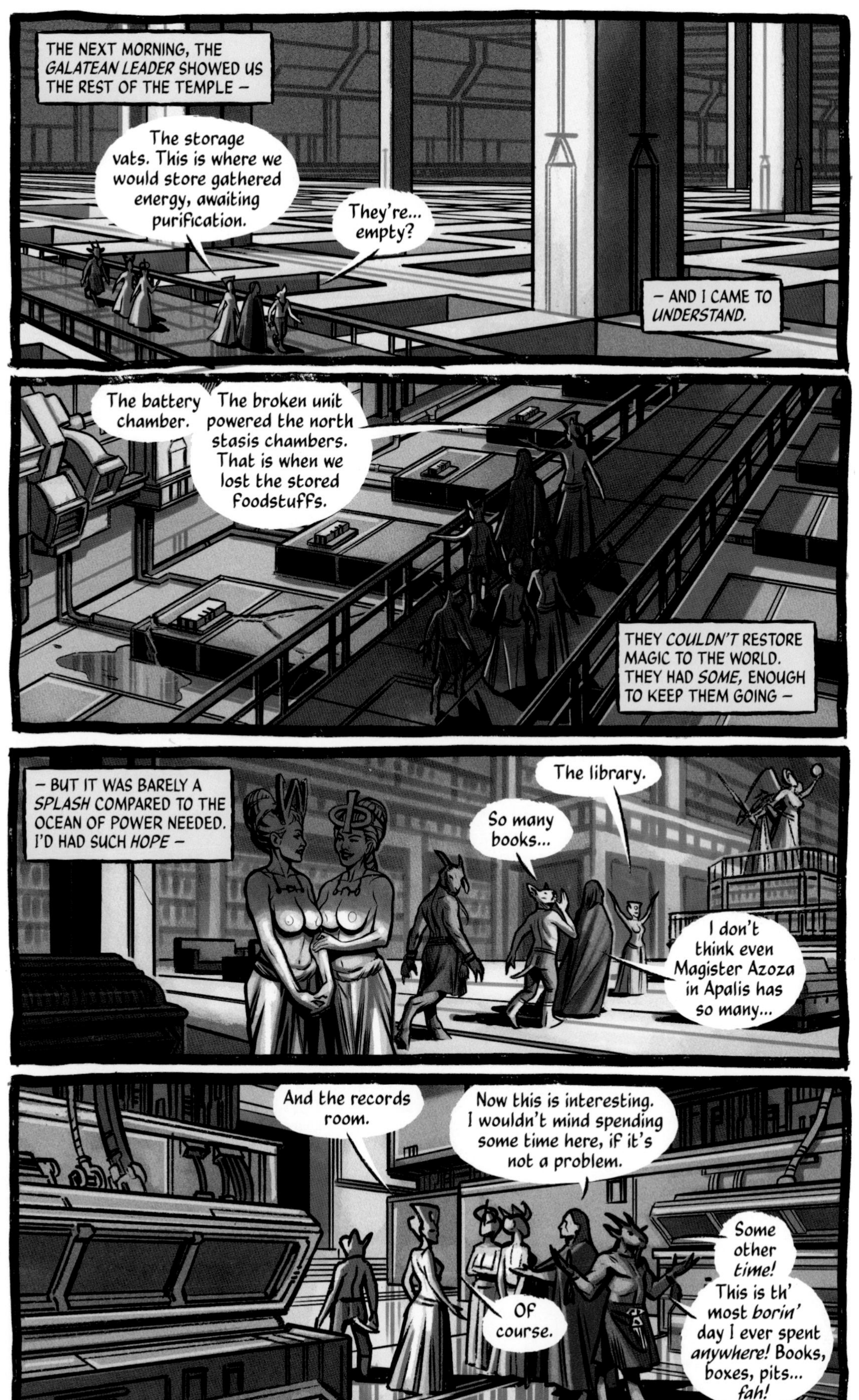
THE NEXT MORNING, THE *GALATEAN LEADER* SHOWED US THE REST OF THE TEMPLE –
The storage vats. This is where we would store gathered energy, awaiting purification.
They're... empty?
– AND I CAME TO *UNDERSTAND.*
The battery chamber.
The broken unit powered the north stasis chambers. That is when we lost the stored foodstuffs.
THEY *COULDN'T* RESTORE MAGIC TO THE WORLD. THEY HAD *SOME*, ENOUGH TO KEEP THEM GOING –
– BUT IT WAS BARELY A *SPLASH* COMPARED TO THE OCEAN OF POWER NEEDED. I'D HAD SUCH *HOPE* –
The library.
So many books...
I don't think even Magister Azoza in Apalis has so many...
And the records room.
Now this is interesting. I wouldn't mind spending some time here, if it's not a problem.
Of course.
Some other *time!* This is th' most *borin'* day I ever spent *anywhere!* Books, boxes, pits... *fah!*

THE DAY WAS *MILD*, SO THEY OFFERED TO SERVE OUR EVENING MEAL *OUTSIDE* –
Wa-hey!

Learoyd? What's wrong?
Jesus shit, kid, what isn't?
What *isn't*?

These women... statues, androids, Galateans, whatever the fuck. Maybe they were machines when they started out, but now...
They think. They feel. They're capable of fucking *choice*.
And to live like this and then just *die*...
...no one should have to endure this. *No one*.
IT WAS THE FIRST TIME I'D *SEEN* HIM LIKE THAT...

Hoi! Come an' eat – afore I scarfs th' *lot!*
...CONCERNED, ANGRY, BUT FOR SOMEONE *OTHER* THAN HIMSELF.
IN KENEIL, HE WAS SAVING *HIMSELF* ALONG WITH US. AND THERE WERE CLEARLY THINGS HE WANTED TO *LEARN* HERE, BUT HIS MOOD...IT WAS *NEW*.

THE NEXT MORNING, THEY BEGAN TO SHOW US THE *GROUNDS*, BUT –
Enough o' this! I been seein' fackin' hills an' dirt all my life!
These two nannies are gonna gi' me a cheese an' beer an' uiskay tour, hey? Aren't you, darlins?
Fine – but you fuckin' leave 'em *alone*, Bertie, you hear me?
Wa-*hey*!
This fuckin' world.
I thought it was a dream, at first. It comes off goofy, all badgers and warthogs in fancy robes and shit. Like a kids' story.
But there's just as much shit here as there is *anywhere*, isn't there?
Master Stephen?
Did you want to see the records room again?
Just... Learoyd.
None of this "master" shit. I'm not your master.

But fuck what *I* want.
What do you...hang on a minute.
Do you even have a name?
What do I call you?
Jesus, what a
shithead.
Different masters
assigned us different
names, according to their
preference. The first
master sometimes liked
to call me Eliza...

But okay. Eliza.
What do *you* want,
Eliza?
Fuck duties.
Fuck orders.
What do *you*
want to do with
your days? With
your *life?*

I...

I honestly cannot say I have ever
given the question any thought.
This is the first time anyone
has asked it.
We
had our
duties...
Yeah? Well, maybe
you should think
about it now,
lady.
I mean...
...before you up
and blow yourself to
shit because no one's
updated your to-do
list lately.
No tasks. Just life.
Your choice, all of it.
Would you even
want that?

I...would have to ponder that. Discuss it with my sisters. No tasks? Just life?
Would we still...please men?
Not unless you wanted to. It'd be your choice. No one gets to command you to do anything.
No one.
My choice...?
Wa-HEYY...
Are you happy, Master Bertie? Hungry? Thirsty?
Is your appetite slaked?
I'm good, nans, I'm good.
But henryhiggins, henryhiggins, ye gotta do what I *say*, aye? That's th' *deal*, yeah?
'Cause I got me a new command for *all* of ye...

WHKROOM
Wh-huh?

That was the temple!
What's going on?

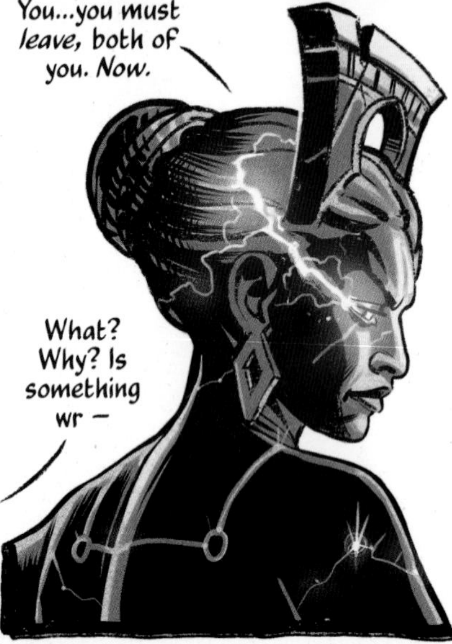
You...you must *leave*, both of you. *Now.*
What? Why? Is something wr —

Leave *now* and never *return.*
You are *no masters.* You have never *been* masters. You are *deceivers.* And we cannot *tolerate* deceivers.
You should — you *must* be —

GO!
I should *destroy* you — my *orders* are to destroy you — but I — for the *kindnesses* you have shown, I — I wish —
Please go! Go before I *must* —

But I don't underst –

Not now, kid.

There's a time for talk and a time for gettin' the fuck out of Dodge.

You can understand *later.*

Eliza wouldn't... she wouldn't *hurt* us...

You don't fuckin' *know* what she'd do. I don't think *she* knows, right now. She was *controlling* herself, but the strain –

– she doesn't want to hurt *anyone,* but if she built up enough pressure she might even –

WHROMM
KRAMM

Learoyd, the temple!
Ah, shit...

Learoyd, *Bertie's* in there!

That looks interesting...

Seven

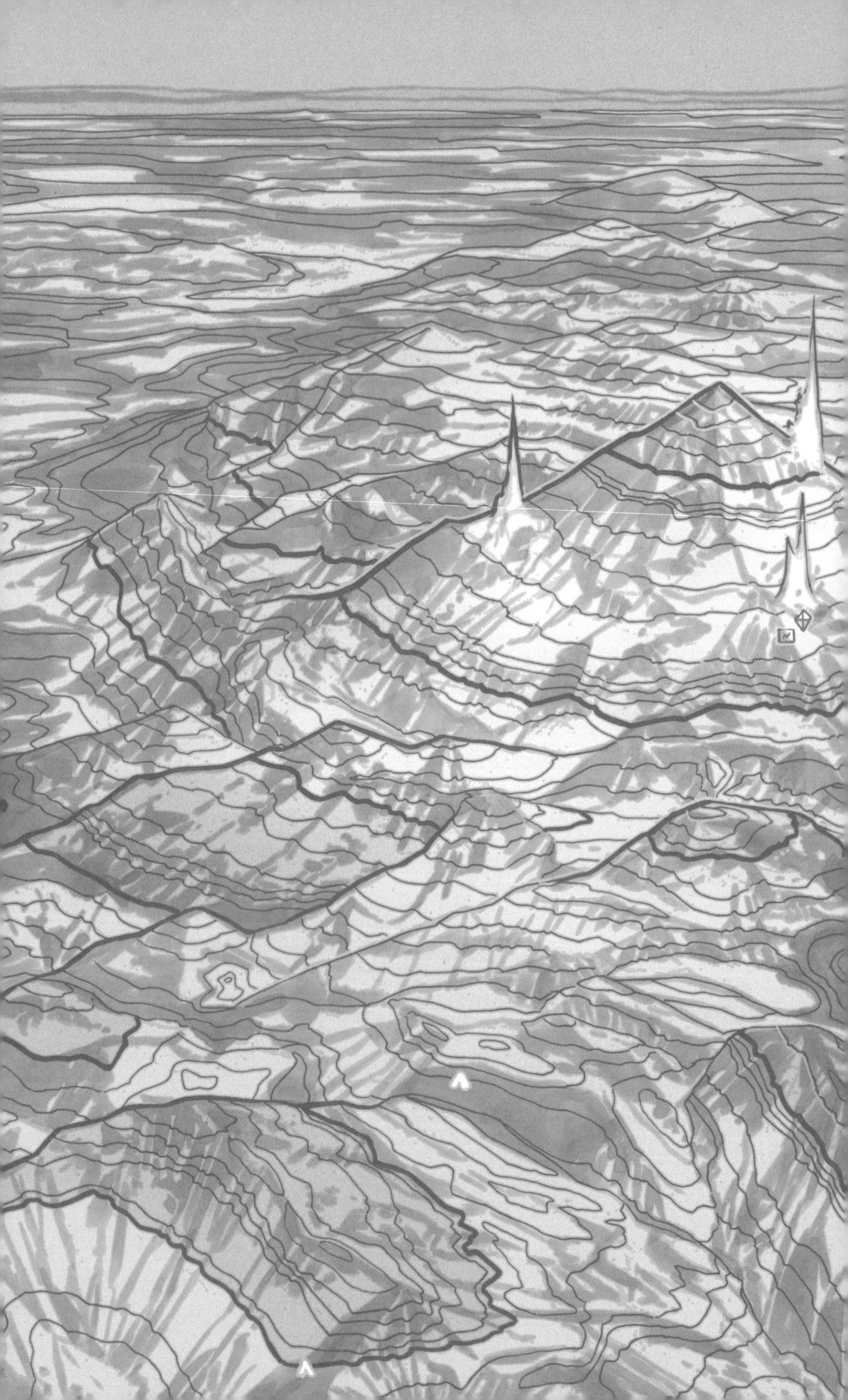

BZEET DEET?
No, gamma-rho, not yet.
Start unit construction and pre-deployment, but this shouldn't be happening. I want to observe a bit before –
Hm? What in the Esoteric – ?
DLIT?
Down there. Three clicks ahead.
The young terrier – long way from home, that one – but the chap he's with –
– that's one of McCready's. I met him. What's he up to here?
And why is it I can see him just fine with the naked eye, but the scanners – even the visual scanners –
– show nothing but footprints?
What is going on here?

THE TEMPLE SHONE with the light of welcome.

All was prepared. All was prepared, as it had been decreed.

The granddaughters of Feniz, Goddess of Energy, took their responsibilities seriously, performing them dutifully and well. That which the goddess wished, they made reality.

And a visit from their grandmother-goddess-that was honor and majesty, a gift from abov All must be made clean and new and shining wit welcome on such an occasion, and so it had been

The goddess, not long before, had grante succor to the Great Champion in the wake of hi battle with the army of the treacherous biso Seven-Scars, blessing him with food, clothin

nd the healing of his wounds. And surely she lessed him with knowledge, as well, for he and is companions found their way to the last Temple f the Sun, which no living creature had seen since efore the tribes first arose in the Vernal Lands.

And as obedient granddaughters, the Galitaan ad welcomed them as heroes errant and servants f the gods, giving them honor, rest, comfort and a surcease from danger.

But now it was time to sally forth once more. Now it was time for the Champion and his band to be given their new quest, and the Galitaan the thanks of their father-mother for their eons of faithful service.

The temple shone with welcome...

Could — could he still be alive in there? Could anyone?
Fuck if I know, Dusty. It doesn't look good, that's for sure.
But hell...

...there's only one ≡nnh!≡ way to find out!

INSIDE, IF ANYTHING, THE TEMPLE WAS WORSE.
He said he was goin' in for food an' booze. But if I know Bertie at all, he wouldn't be in the dining hall.
The pillow rooms were down there...
AND AS I WONDERED IF ANY OF US WOULD LIVE TO MAKE IT BACK OUT —

You.

You are not masters. You are deceivers.
Eliza has given the order. You are no longer welcome here. You must leave — or be destroyed.

Yeah?
Try it, toots.

Um. Excuse me.
We'll be gone as soon as we can.

WE PASSED THE *DINING HALLS* ALONG THE WAY, AND SURE ENOUGH, THERE WAS *NO SIGN* OF BERTIE.
THE GALATEANS HAD BEEN SHOWING US THE *TEMPLE GROUNDS,* BUT HE'D GROWN *TIRED* OF IT, AND GONE IN WITH A COUPLE OF THEM FOR FOOD.
LEAROYD HAD WARNED HIM NOT TO *MOLEST* THEM, BUT I WONDERED –

Always in the fuckin' pillow rooms. I knew it...
Bertie! You still breathing?
hhnh...

F-fer...fer now, but not...much longer...
This's the end...fer Dirty Aelbert o' the Hardhill Clan...lived free...bowed horns t'no...
Eulogize yourself later, guy. What happened?

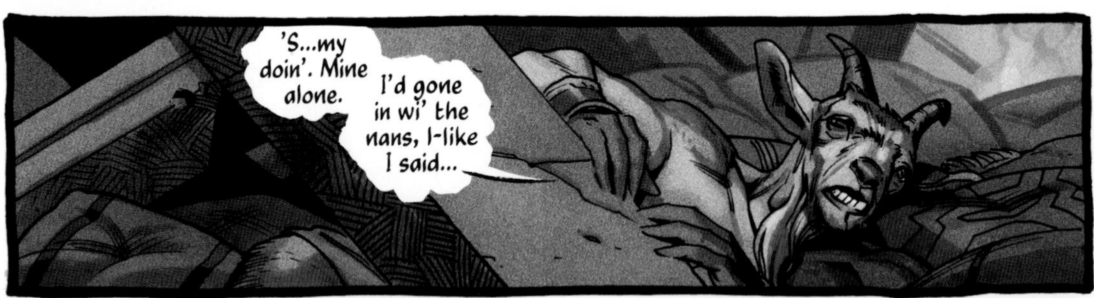
'S...my doin'. Mine alone.
I'd gone in wi' the nans, l-like I said...

"THEY FED ME, BROUGHT ME TH' GOOD STUFF T'DRINK..."
Are you happy, Master Bertie? Hungry? Thirsty?
Your appetite slaked?
I'm good, nans, I'm good. But *henryhiggins, henryhiggins,* you gotta do what I say, eh? That's th' deal, yeah?

'Cause me I got a new command fer ye. For what ye did to th' Craglanders...
...ye're to *destroy* each other!
No *mercy,* no *peaceful death!* Do it *hard!* Make it *hurt!*

You...
You are no *master!*

The masters do not give prohibited commands!
None of you are masters! You are deceivers!

I will disintegrate hi—

"I DIDN'T KNOW WHAT T'*DO.* SO I JUST TRIED T' GET IN CLOSE, *TRIPPED* 'ER..."

ZKAKK

"I GUESS IT HIT SOMETHIN' *IMPORTANT.* THEIR LIGHTNIN' STORAGE TANKS OR *WHATE'ER* IT WAS.
"AN' ME, I WAS SCRAMBLIN' FOR *COVER,* BUT –"

AAAH!

I ain't g-gonna...make it. How w-was I t'know there was...stuff they wouldn't d-do?
B-but I... lived free. B-bowed no horns...
The power storage vats are *empty*, as we showed you.
It was the battery chambers. The blast set off a *chain reaction*.
I told you to go.

Yeah, you did. And I understand why.
But look, you knew we'd have to —

Shut up.

You intend to reason at me. To explain why we should do what *you* think most useful. But that is *not* your choice.
Our duties tell us to *destroy* you. If we follow them, then *that* is what we should do.
You have said that our duties are *over*, that we should choose for *ourselves*, do what *we* want.
If we do that, *we* decide. *Not* you.

Either way, you do *not* choose.
The masters do. Or *we* do.

...
Yeah.

Choose, then.

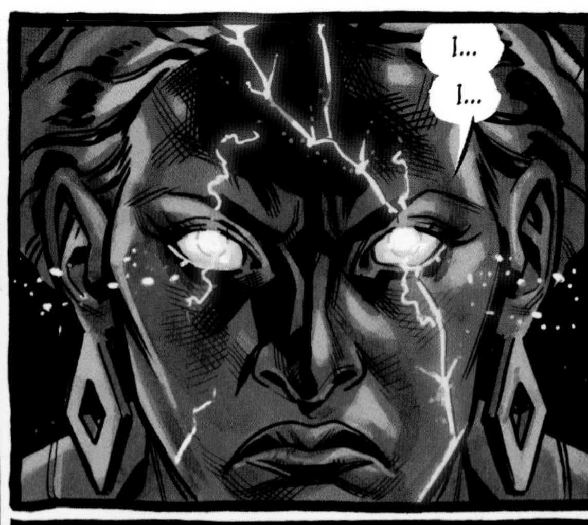
I...
I...

You damaged us, goat. But we'd damaged you first, inadvertently, harming those of your race you call the Craglanders.
We understand revenge. We have read of it in books, heard of it in music.

But go.
You will not be allowed the chance to damage us again.
He could use a little medical attention. He's got broken bones, internal injuries...

Our medical bays are buried, deceiver.
And even if they weren't, I would not –

RMMMBBE
Eh?
Above.

WE CLIMBED BACK OUT AS FAST AS WE *COULD*, AND –
≡nnh≡
S-so what's... the...?
Unit construction: 27%.
Her again?
Och, I dinna...
Huh?
Oh my – oh!
Praise the gods! Praise Idente!

What are you *seeing*, kid? Describe it.
It's... palaces above, it's...

A bird... a blazing, wondrous bird...
It's her. *Feniz.*
Goddess of Energy. But the gods haven't been seen, haven't even spoken in hundreds of years...

Ye-ye're blind, dogpup. She's a g-goat.
A-all th' gods're goats...

Are you a master?
Oh, good grief. "Henry Higgins."
That idiotic Pierson and his idiotic codewords...

And you.
I've got a minor leak here, and go off to do some cleanup to the northeast — and you turn it into a full-on disaster.
Unit construction: 41%.

Who *are* you, anyway?
And why don't you show up on any of our sensors?
You wanna know?

Then I'm going to need some fuckin' answers, *here.*
About this installation, about these statue-women. You tell me what I want to know, and I'll —

How...utterly brazen. *This* is what passes for interdeity espionage these days?
Never mind. I don't need answers from *you.* I'll just buzz your boss, McCready —

— and ask him about your corpse!

AH!
AHH!

...in the name of sixteen goddamn conga-dancing shits was THAT?!
He's... alive?
Look, lady, I don't know who the hell you think you are, but –
He's still alive!
You're...not with McCready, are you?

Yeah, you never *asked*, did you? You barely even let me get a word in *edgewise.* Did I ever *say* I was with McCready?
Whoever the fuck *that* is.

Do I need to point out that that's not really an *answer?*

Well, *boo* fuckin' *hoo.*
I'm in the dark on plenty of stuff myself, so maybe we can scratch each other's back. First, though, you could *help out* around here a little bit.
Help... out?
This is starting to feel *surreal.* What did you have in mind, O enigmatic one?

The goat.
Back when we met and you gave me the nice outfit you just fried to shit, you tried to fix my shoulder.
Think you can fix his injuries?

Pff. Of course. Beta-beta! Gamma-tau! Full scan and repairs on that one.
BZZ ZZT
uhh...

But why even ask? It's just one goat.
A friend of mine once said, "Because we can," but somehow I think that'd fall on deaf ears.
So instead, how about... humor me.

Very well. But I still don't —
Unit construction: 78%.
Thank you, great one. *Thank you!*
Your benevolence is *unparalleled,* your power *unending...*

What the fuck? Dusty, get up.
Why even *do* that? She's no goddess, and she's certainly not —
He does not hear what you hear, any more than he sees what you see.

Neither from me, nor you.
What he hears is the *godspeech.* I have no idea why it doesn't work on you, if you're not with Interior.
Is there another *pantheon?*

Maybe. It depends. How many are there supposed to be?
≷sigh≶
Very well, we'll start smaller. What is your name and who are you with?
Learoyd, Stephen T.

And I guess I'm with the pup. Maybe the goat, too. And as long as you're fixing *him*...
...how about them?
The Galateans? You *are* a curious man. Whatever *for?*

They're old. Worn, cracked. They're basically holding off catastrophic failure by sheer willpower, and they're giving up.
They deserve better. You can spackle 'em up, or something, right?

Of course I could. But there'd be no point to that, Mister Learoyd.
Why not?

This installation is *long* past its era of usefulness.
It should have been shut down *millennia* ago, but there were...those who found it *relaxing.* Idiots.
I'd forgotten it until the leak. Now I'm here to decommission the entire facility.

And when I'm done, trust me...
Unit construction: 100%.

...there really won't be anything left behind to *repair*.

Eight

What — what are they saying?
They disagree about us.
About what our fate is to be.
THEY TALKED IN *GODSPEECH.* I HAD NO IDEA LEAROYD EVEN *UNDERSTOOD* GODSPEECH, MUCH LESS COULD RESPOND.
AND I WONDERED, NOT FOR THE FIRST TIME — THE GREAT CHAMPION, *GODS* — WHAT HAD MY LIFE *BECOME?*

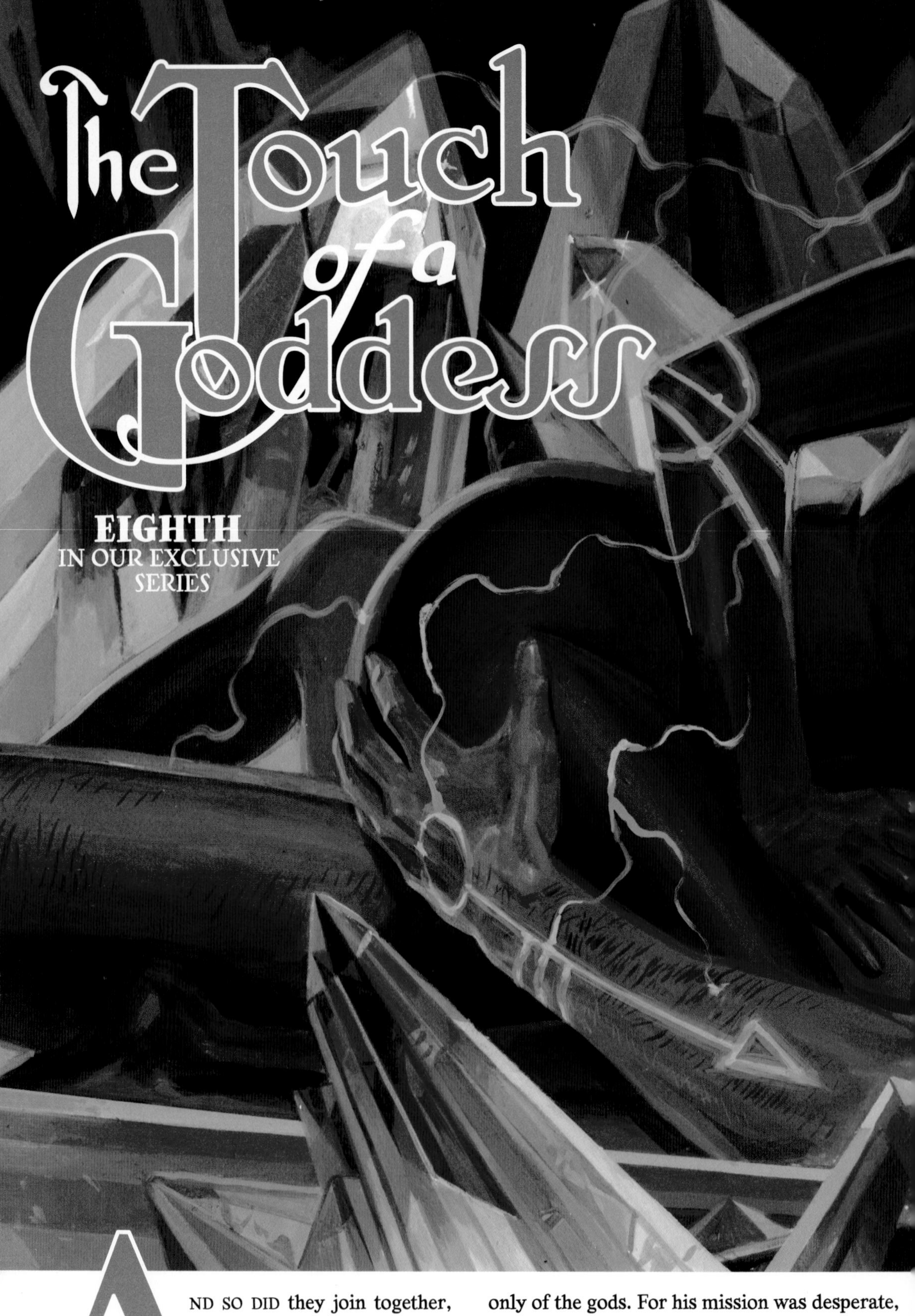

AND SO DID they join together, goddess and champion, sharing passion, essence and spirit.

Feniz came to him in a form like unto his, to affirm his mission and share her power. To remake him from the heart outward, granting him miraculous abilities that are the province only of the gods. For his mission was desperate, and her need of a champion—*our* need of a champion—great.

Male and female did they join, tan and copper, enveloping, driving, commingling, their spasms shaking the hills and their gasps echoing across the sky. Heroic might thrust through, godly power drew in, in a shuddering, ecstatic

conjoining that saw the Champion glimpse the divine and the goddess feel the breathless cry of mortality.

For was he not *her* Champion? Was she not the *reason* for all he did, the reason he existed at all?

He came to the Temple of the Sun, this we know. He met a goddess there. He displayed miraculous power. How then, could it be otherwise? She gave him a piece of her heart. He took her desires as his command. He came to be succored by her granddaughters, the Galitaan, and she blessed him.

The heretics say different, but the heretics lie. There was no battle. How *could* there have been? Even a Champion cannot challenge a god.

Fuck *you*, lady! **FUCK YOU!**
These women served you — served you well! They shouldn't be killed just because you don't have a use for them any more!
They're not women. They're machines.
And if I say they're done, they're done. How are you going to stop me?
KTOW

Why, you –
You –
I *was* going to take you back with me. I *was* going to treat you like an equal. Or at *least* a valuable curiosity.
But now?

To *hell* with you! *To hell with you!* I'll flay your *flesh* from your *bones,* and let the *analysts* sort it out!
Because I. Will. Not. Be. Touched!

AND THERE – THERE WAS *SO MUCH* HATSAS – I COULDN'T *IMAGINE* SO MUCH –

BUT –
I DIDN'T *UNDERSTAND.* NOT WHY HE WOULD *FIGHT* A GODDESS –
How – how did he – ?
NOT HOW HE COULD *SURVIVE* A GODDESS –

This is *absurd!*
My lightning didn't work on you.
Sheer *pranic force* didn't work on you. Why won't you *die?* Why are you *invisible* to my scanners?

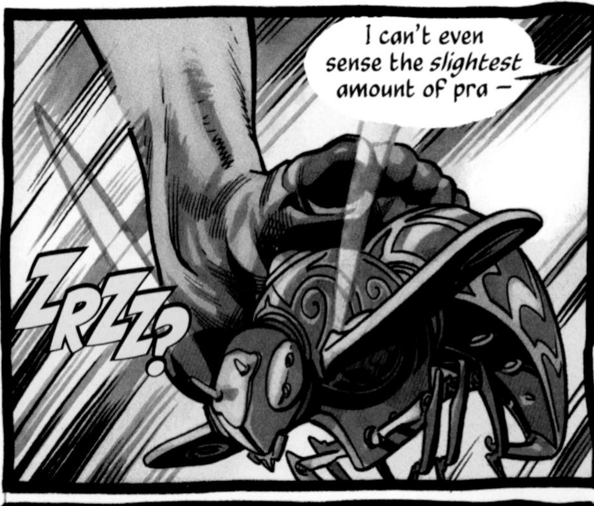
I can't even sense the *slightest* amount of pra –
ZRZZ?!

Wh – ?

I DIDN'T EVEN UNDERSTAND WHY HE WAS LIKE THIS *AT ALL.* HE'D SEEMED TO ME *COLD,* CALCULATING –
– A WARRIOR WHO DIDN'T FIGHT WITHOUT A *PLAN,* WITHOUT SOME *BENEFIT* HE COULD SEE FOR HIMSELF –

AIHH –
AND YET HERE HE *WAS* –

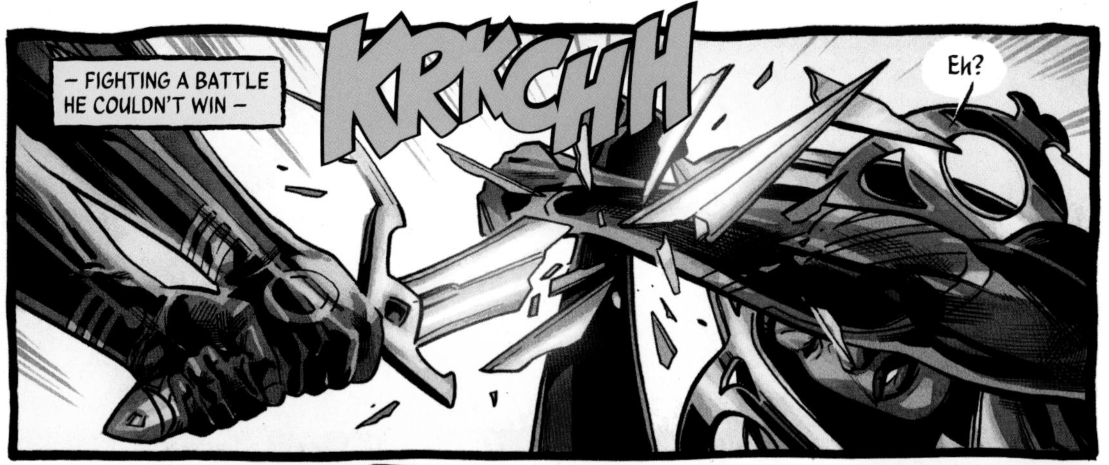

– FIGHTING A BATTLE HE COULDN'T WIN –
KRKCHH
Eh?

– FOR UNLIVING BEINGS WHO DIDN'T *ASK* HIS HELP –
HNHH!
KRKT

Wait, wait. You don't – magic doesn't work against you. My protections don't work against you.
No. And if you don't leave this place –

But they worked against your sword.
Maybe...

RRRRRRRRMMMMMMMMMBBBLLLLL
Ah hah.
WHY DID HE *FIGHT* FOR THEM? I DIDN'T *KNOW.*

I DIDN'T THINK, BACK THEN, I EVER WOULD. OF COURSE, AT THAT *MOMENT* –
Ah-*hah!*
Hh – ?
Ah, shit.
Magic doesn't work on you. I don't know why. But it works on things *around* you. And physical objects affect you just fine.
So, Steven T. Learoyd, you *do* get to discover after all –
WHRMM
– what it means to offend a goddess!
– I DIDN'T EXPECT HIM TO *SURVIVE.*

I THINK, PERHAPS, HE VERY NEARLY *DIDN'T.*
WHUMPPP

Galateans. Take him inside and secure him. *Guard* him. It seems I'll be taking him with me when I depart after all.
But first, I have to clean up this *ridiculous mess* you and Pierson created.
Should have wiped this peak clean centuries ago...

THEY TOOK US WITHIN WHAT *REMAINED* OF THE TEMPLE. AND THEN THEY DID NOTHING. THEY JUST *WATCHED.*

I WANTED TO SHOUT AT THEM, TO *HOWL.* HOW COULD THEY *DO* THIS? SHE WOULD KILL THEM *ALL!* HOW COULD THEY GO TO THEIR DEATHS SO *PLACIDLY?*

HE HAD FOUGHT FOR THEM! WHY DIDN'T THEY FIGHT FOR THEMSELVES?

BUT I DIDN'T DO ANYTHING *EITHER.* I JUST WATCHED LEAROYD BREATHE. *SHALLOWLY,* AND WITH PAINFUL TWITCHES.

BROKEN RIBS, I REALIZED. I THOUGHT TO *HEAL* THEM, USING THE COPIOUS AMBIENT HATSAS...

I don't like this.
We were fine. We had our duty, we had our orders. We would have gone to our termination without complaint. We did not ask for anything.
C-can scatter... head for cover in small groups...
Only one of h-her. Can't d-divide efforts. Robots can be d-dealt with.
She'll g-get some. But others...some will escape...
Damn you!
We were *fine*! We did not *ask* you!
Perhaps...perhaps he did not do it for us.
Yes. Much of the literature we studied is of noble, self-sacrificing heroism. But some...
Perhaps he did it for himself.
Perhaps his own code would not let him stand by, and thus be complicit in her deeds?
COULD THAT BE *IT?* I REALLY DIDN'T KNOW. I HAD COME TO UNDERSTAND THAT WE CAME HERE LOOKING FOR *ANSWERS.*
ABOUT THE AUTUMNLANDS *THEMSELVES,* THEIR HISTORY, THEIR WORKINGS. ANSWERS I COULDN'T *GIVE* HIM, BECAUSE ALL I KNEW WERE LEGENDS.

I'D EVEN THOUGHT *HIM* TO BE A LEGEND.
Whatever his reasons, they cannot be ours. We choose for ourselves.
So choose. Do you wish to defy our duty? To disobey? To live?

IT WAS ALWAYS *STRANGE,* TO SEE THEM COMMUNICATE SILENTLY...
...*HOWEVER* IT WAS THAT THEIR ARTIFICIAL CREATION LET THEM *DO* IT.

AND IN THE *END* –
Very well.
Then Learoyd is correct. Our best results will come if we scatter, while a few sacrifice ourselves to occupy her.
I shall confront her. Any others who –

No, Eliza.
No, sister.
You have done enough for us.

Come.
Huh?

Here.
This will allow you to depart.

The tunnel will take you to a maintenance exit very close to the treeline.
We hope he is correct about your chances, and that you live.

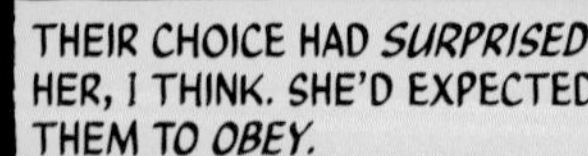
THEIR CHOICE HAD *SURPRISED* HER, I THINK. SHE'D EXPECTED THEM TO *OBEY.*

SO *MANY* PEOPLE EXPECT OTHERS TO OBEY. I THINK THAT WAS THE FIRST TIME I *ASKED* MYSELF: WHAT HAPPENS IF THEY *DON'T?*

WHAT HAPPENS IF THE *WORLD* DOESN'T?
So. We are prepared.
On my signal, initiate erasu –
WHRAM
WHRAM
WHRAM
Eh?
What in – ?
This is rank disobedience! Henryhiggins! Henryhiggins! Stop this at once!

SHRAMM
UHH - !
SHRAMM

Madness! He's infected you with –

No! Don't you –
Now, sister!
For *Eliza!* For us *all!*

WHRAM
WHRTAMM

Come, sister.
We must go now.

Yes. We must not waste their sacrifice.
I hear them as they die. I hear their final thoughts.
I hear them telling us what we must do.

Holy gods above. Holy *Idente* above all — !
You're...still keeping that cleanse spell going, Dusty? Protecting yourself and Bertie from all this?
Yes. We're clean.
Are... are they winning?
No.

NNN-RAHH!
And that... is *that!* All *units!* Repair and *rebuild!* With *all deliberate speed!*
Rebuild *now!*
We should go. Get under cover, make some distance while we can.
Right.
Bertie, when we stop for the night, I can heal your leg further...
Nah.
Them buzzin' beasts fixed up my innards, I'm good. I'll heal up normal. Hardhill Clan, y'ken?
I'm goin' back. Down where I belong. But y'ever need me, just call. I'll come runnin'.
Thank you. And can you tell the sheepfolk — their water should be clean in, ah, a week, maybe two?
Aye, I'll do that.
I'll tell 'em the tale.
THE *TALE.*
WE WERE GOING TO BE IN *TALES,* I REALIZED. SOMETHING *ELSE* I'D NEVER EXPECTED.

Damn, damn, damn.
Three days' work, even at top speed. Repairs, erasure, cleaning this place, purifying the toxins out of the system.
But that Learoyd...
I can't track him, Gamma-rho. No sign of him at all. And I didn't think to tag the goat or the pup.
They'll vanish in the general mammal signals.
Still, we'll be on the lookout. Whatever he is, he can't stay in the shadows forever.
And at least the Galateans have finally been disposed of.
What do you think they said to her, Learoyd?
The other Galateans? To keep her from sacrificing herself?
I was pretty out of it, kid. I have no idea...

Live, sister.
Live for us.

To be continued...

ISSUE 7 COVER SKETCHES.

E

F

C
D
Autumnlands
6
Autumnlands
TOOTH & CLAW
H

COVER DESIGNS

Our usual cover process:

Kurt and Ben talk over concepts.

Ben goes absolutely batshit with his sketchbook and works up a bunch of amazing designs, all of which look great.

Kurt and Ben talk over the designs. Where the text will fit, what elements are emphasized, are there story surprises, like that.

Ben kicks ass drawing and toning.

Jordie kicks ass coloring, bringing Ben's work to an even higher level.

JG kicks ass on the text design.

BOOM. Done. Next?